CHRISTMAS CRACKERS

CHERRY COBB
TIM GAMBRELL
TERRY COOPER
KEREN WILLIAMS
CHRIS LYNCH

CANDY JAR BOOKS · CARDIFF
2022

Range Editor: Shaun Russell
Edited by Will Rees & Keren Williams
Continuity Editor: Andy Frankham-Allen
Cover: Steve Beckett
Licensed by Hannah Haisman

Published by
Candy Jar Books
Mackintosh House
136 Newport Road, Cardiff, CF24 1DJ
www.candyjarbooks.co.uk

CONTENTS

THE MOBILE ARMY

Cherry Cobb

Lucy was up and out of bed by seven o'clock on Saturday morning, despite the icy frost lacing her bedroom window and the sub-zero temperatures outside. The weather in Ogmore-by-Sea was a lot colder than it had been in London; the bitter wind could freeze your fingers faster than an ice cream freezes your brain. Shivering, she slid open her chest of drawers in search of something warm to wear. She didn't want to be late on the day of the school Christmas Fayre. She and Hobo were helping out. Digging out a woolly jumper, she headed downstairs.

'What are you looking for?' Mum asked as Lucy ferreted about in the under-stairs cupboard for her favourite red jacket.

'Where's my coat?' Lucy raked through the hangers, knocking jackets and scarves to the floor. 'And my scarf. I've lost my scarf.'

'Lucy Wilson, stop that right now,' said Mum, glaring. 'Your coat is exactly where you left it. Hanging over the back of the kitchen chair. Oh, and I'm sure you'll have a new scarf for Christmas.'

'Sorry, Mum. Thanks.' Lucy gave her a quick hug.

Mum rolled her eyes. 'Kids,' she muttered under her breath.

Lucy ran and got her coat, before picking up the boxes of crackers Mum had got from the cash and carry for them to sell at the fayre.

Lucy examined the crackers inside the clear plastic.

There were several little holes in the tubes, like something had burst out!

'Mum, have we got mice?' she asked.

'I hope not.'

'But look at these crackers.' She showed her the box.

'It's probably a faulty batch. The gunpowder or something.'

'I don't think they actually use gunpowder, Mum.' She looked at the saucepan bubbling like a witch's cauldron.

'What's that? Look's nice.'

'It's chilli for tea,' said Mum. 'Hobo is welcome to stay.'

Lucy gave her a winning smile. 'He'd like that. I think his mum is working late tonight. I expect we'll stay behind and help clear up though.'

Hobo was busy in the school hall helping to set out the tables when Lucy arrived. She placed the boxes of crackers on the stage and removed her gloves.

'Phew, it's warm in here,' she said.

Hobo grinned. 'Hopefully it will encourage people to stay. I really hope we can raise some money for the Children from Chernobyl charity. If they get enough money throughout the year they bring some of the kids over for a holiday. They might even come to Wales.' He beamed. 'Lots of them don't have any hair

2

either because of the high levels of radiation in their town.' He rubbed his head ruefully.

Hobo had got used to the sarcastic comments and bullying about his alopecia over the years, but hated to think of others who might not be strong enough to stand up for themselves.

'I know.' Lucy gave his arm a squeeze. She too had experienced bullying due to being mixed-race. She knew how much it meant to Hobo to try and help the Ukrainian kids born in the aftermath of a nuclear fallout.

'We'd better get our table sorted and see if anyone else needs a hand,' she said checking the time.

They busied themselves with setting up the stall. Hobo set out the prizes on the shelf behind them, while Lucy covered the table with a red cloth decorated with white snowflakes and snowmen, before laying out a stack of Christmas crackers in red, gold and green. She carefully marked some of them with the point of her red pen. These crackers had an extra prize. The others still had the usual joke, hat and toy, so everyone won something.

'I'll go and get us a drink each from the canteen before we officially open,' said Hobo, shouting above the sudden burst of Christmas music blaring out from the speakers. Mr Jolly, the music teacher, rushed across the hall with his hands over his ears.

'I hope he sorts that out,' shouted Lucy. 'Or we'll

all be hoarse by the end of the day.'

As Lucy finished off the stall she inhaled the delicious smell of cinnamon and ginger coming from the kitchen where they were baking cookies in readiness for a big crowd. She gazed around the hall, which was decorated with a mass of coloured paper chains, tinsel and garlands. There were festive stickers stuck on the doors and fake snow on the windows. A large tree draped with twinkling lights stood in the centre of the stage. Lucy loved Christmas, the crisp mornings and the deep snow that fell in Ogmore-by-Sea. It had never been like that in London. They were lucky to get enough to make a snowman.

The hall was rapidly filling up with volunteers laying out tables filled with stuffed toys, fancy soaps, handmade jewellery, and other gifts to entice people to part with their money. The tombola stall practically groaned with the weight of all the cakes, chocolates and mulled wine that had been donated as raffle prizes.

One of the teachers was pinning up posters advertising Santa's grotto, which had been set up in one of the smaller classrooms, transformed for the day into a winter wonderland.

Lucy rubbed her hands together; it was going to be a good Christmas, she could feel it in her bones, and for once there wasn't an alien in sight. She busied herself finishing off the stall and placing a box for rubbish by the side of the table. Out of the corner of her eye she noticed something move. Was it a mouse? Had she brought one with her from home?

'Here you go.' Hobo passed her a paper cup filled to the brim with hot chocolate and a pink marshmallow floating on top. 'It's starting to look really Christmassy in here,' he said.

'I notice that Mel and her crowd aren't helping,' said Lucy.

'The best help she can offer would be to stay away,' said Hobo firmly. He tried not to dislike anyone but it proved challenging with Mel.

'We can only hope,' Lucy replied, rolling her eyes. 'Do you think we have enough crackers?' Her eyes scanned the table.

'I think the PTA have some more. I'm sure I saw someone bringing a load in from their car. We could always use those if we run out,' Hobo said, blowing on his drink. 'How much are we supposed to charge?'

'One pound. I'll write it on a piece of paper and stick it on the front of the desk.' Lucy dived into her bag for a Sharpie. 'Oh, I forgot to mention, Mum's cooking chilli tonight. She said you're welcome to stay if you fancy it?'

Hobo's eyes lit up. 'You bet. It beats eating a cold floppy sandwich from the fridge.'

'Is your mum coming?' she said as she fiddled with the sticky tape.

5

'She's going to try and pop in before she goes to work.'

Lucy could hear a slow hum of chatter coming from the doors on the other side of the hall. *That's a good sign*, Lucy thought, glancing at the clock.

'Five minutes everyone,' called Mr Thomas. 'We will have a countdown for the last minute. The first person through the door gets a free go on the tombola.'

There was a frantic scrabble as everyone finished off their stalls and quickly got behind their tables.

A few minutes later, Mr Thomas pulled open the double doors to the hall.

'Welcome everyone to our annual Christmas Fayre, and a big thank you for coming. Our charity this year is in aid of the Children from Chernobyl. We hope to pass on some of our profits, so dig deep and don't leave empty handed.' He smiled. 'Let the countdown begin! Five. Four. Three. Two. One! 'Happy shopping!'

Everybody cheered. Lucy and Hobo watched as people swarmed into the hall.

'Good luck,' said Hobo, as he passed Lucy the reindeer headbands they'd agreed to wear.

'Thanks,' said Lucy, grinning.

Lucy and Hobo were kept busy with lots of parents with small children wanting to pull the crackers and win a prize.

'Oh, look it's Santa's little helpers selling crackers,'

snorted Mel as she walked by with her groupies.

'At least we're doing something, unlike some,' Lucy snapped. 'How much have you raised, Mel?'

Mel's face flushed red like Rudolph's nose. 'Maybe you should raise money for a wig for your monkey,' she spat.

Lucy flew out from behind the table, 'You take that back, right now.'

Hobo grabbed Lucy's arm. 'Leave it, Lucy. You know she's only trying to wind you up.' He pulled her back around the table.

Lucy breathed deeply. She pictured Grandad nodding his approval. 'Be the bigger person, Lucy,' she muttered to herself.

'Can I have two crackers please?'

Lucy looked up to see Mrs Kostinen standing in front of the stall.

'Hi, Mum, thanks for coming,' said Hobo.

'Hello, Mrs Kostinen, come to try for the winning prize?' Lucy gestured to the array of prizes lined up behind her.

'I've just won a bottle of mulled wine on the tombola so you never know.' She handed over a two pound coin. 'I'll pull one with each of you,' she said holding up two gold crackers.

With a firm pull on the crackers two plastic men with parachutes tied around their waists burst out. Lucy watched as one of them appeared to move its head.

'Did you see. that? It moved its head,' said Lucy. She grabbed one the plastic men and held it up to the light. 'I think it's supposed to be a soldier, but it's not been made very well. It only has three fingers.'

'Really? Like cartoon characters,' said Hobo.

'What?'

'Three fingers.'

'What are you on about?'

'Bart Simpson, Mickey Mouse, the Seven Dwarfs, they all have three fingers. Not the Disney princesses though. I've always thought that was strange.'

'Why is this relevant?'

'Don't know, just thought it was interesting.'

Lucy decided to ignore her friend's ramblings. 'Sorry, Mrs Kostinen, better luck next time.'

As Mrs Kostinen drifted away, Lucy started to rifle through the bin.

'Look at this. Why have people been throwing these plastic soldiers away?'

'Dunno. They are pretty hideous.'

'Wouldn't Gav like them?' asked Lucy.

'Probably,' replied Hobo.

The rest of the day went by in a flash. Lucy and Hobo were rushed off their feet right up until four o'clock when the Fayre finished.

'I'm pooped,' Lucy declared, flopping down onto

the stage.

'Me too,' said Hobo. 'But we'd better start packing up. They'll want to lock up soon.'

Lucy agreed and went in search of Mr Thomas to give him the cash they had taken.

Lucy stopped to chat with some of the stall holders, as they packed any remaining goods away.

'Well done, Lucy,' Mr Thomas said as Lucy passed him her money bag. 'You and Hobo have done a fantastic job today. It looks like you raised a fair bit.'

'Thanks, Mr Thomas. It's been a great day.'

'Mr Thomas was pleased with our efforts,' she said, helping Hobo to fold up the table.

'That's great news,' said Hobo. A blast of icy air hit their faces. 'Hey, it's snowing.'

'I'm not surprised, it's freezing out here,' Lucy grumbled as frosted air forced its way into her lungs.

Hobo scooped up some snow and aimed it straight at Lucy.

'Hey cut that out,' she shrieked, as the frozen ball exploded in her face. She spat out a mouthful of cold wet slush.

'Sorry.'

Hobo laughed, looking slightly sheepish.

Lucy put down the box of plastic soldiers for Gav and gathered up handfuls of snow softer than ice, but thicker than soup. She squeezed it into a tight ball and then lobbed it back at Hobo.

'See how you like it,' she said.

Hobo ducked as it sailed past his ear. He picked another snowball and threw it back at her. Before long they were both soaked through.

'Enough,' said Lucy waving her scarf in the air. 'I surrender.'

'Just call me a snow warrior,' said Hobo, smirking. Lucy thought back to the one time she'd had a snowball fight with her dad and brothers. They had considered it great fun to wrestle her to the ground and shove handfuls of freezing snow down her back. She remembered it had taken her ages to warm up afterwards. She had sat in the bath for an hour until her fingers and toes had become wrinkled like the shell of a walnut.

'We'd better get back and dry off. Mum will be dishing up chilli soon,' said Lucy.

Hobo groaned, 'I'm starving, don't talk about food.'

'No change there then,' said Lucy picking up the box of crackers.

Lucy smiled as they crunched though the crystalline snow. She loved the way it laid across the landscape like an unfinished painting – silent and cold. On the rare occasion it had snowed in London it turned to grey, dirty slush within minutes.

She was looking forward to Christmas. Conall,

Dean and Hannah were coming to stay with them and she was going to help Mum make a Christmas cake.

The growl of Hobo's stomach brought her back to reality with a bump. They walked around the back of her house and let themselves into the kitchen.

'Look at the state of you two,' Mum declared, looking at their clothes dripping all over the floor. 'You look like you've both been pulled through a hedge backwards. Go and grab a couple of towels from the bathroom, Lucy, and dry yourselves off. Tea will be ready in ten minutes.' She returned to stirring the large pan of chilli on the hob.

Lucy and Hobo kicked off their shoes and left them by the door with the box of plastic soldiers. Lucy peeled off her coat and hung it on the back of the door. 'Back in a sec,' she said.

Hobo removed his jacket and inhaled the air like a dog sniffing out its favourite bone. 'That smells out of this world, Mrs Wilson,' he said.

'Hi, kids,' said Dad as he strode in, chucking his car keys on the side. 'Something smells good,' he said.

'It's chilli and it's ready now,' Mum replied.

Lucy and Hobo quickly set the table before taking their seats.

'How did the fayre go today?' asked Dad.

'Great,' Lucy mumbled through a mouthful of hot chilli. 'There were lots of people, so hopefully they made a profit.'

'I'll donate a tenner. Got to do my bit,' Dad said.

Lucy licked her lips, 'Thanks, Dad.' Sometimes Dad could really surprise her.

They ate the rest of their food in silence. After the meal, they all went into the lounge to watch TV.

As they all watched the Christmas special *The Billy Bandril Show*, Hobo noticed something move across the room.

'I didn't know you had a cat,' he whispered to Lucy.

'We don't.'

'Really, erm, I'm just going to get a glass of water,' Hobo said, jumping up. He was back in a flash. 'Er, Luce, can you help me find the glasses?'

'You know where we keep them,' said Lucy, giving him a funny look.

'Um, I've forgotten.' He gestured for Lucy to follow him.

Sighing, she pulled herself up off the sofa and followed him into the kitchen.

He shut the door behind her.

'What are you doing?' said Lucy, raising her eyebrows.

'I didn't want to say in front of your parents, but look!'

'Yes, it's the cracker box,' she said looking puzzled.

'It's empty, Lucy!'

'So?'

'Earlier on it had at least twenty toy soldiers in it.'

Lucy grabbed the box and tipped it upside down. Hobo was right. It was empty.

'Maybe Dad emptied the box out?'

Hobo wiped the kitchen window with his hand and peered out into the darkness, using the torch on his phone to illuminate the garden. Suddenly he jumped up and flung open the back door. Lucy followed close on his heels.

There were tiny footprints in the snow leading up the garden path.

'The plastic soldiers!' said Lucy in excitement. 'I knew there was something odd about them.'

'But what are they up to?' asked Hobo.

'I don't know. Let's find out.' Lucy jumped into action, grabbing her coat and shoving her feet back into her wet trainers.

'Hurry, Hobo,' she said as he fumbled with his zip.

Lucy quietly shut the back door behind them. 'That explains the holes in the box.' She kicked at the snow with her shoe, swirling it around like a cloud of ice white dust.

'Stop it, Lucy! We won't be able to follow their tracks.' Hobo shone the torch on his mobile to the ground, and sighed with relief. The footprints were still there.

'Over there!' Hobo pointed. In the distance they could just about make out the small soldiers marching in a line, like a battalion of ants collecting food.

'Where on earth are they going?' muttered Lucy.

'Shh.' Hobo held his finger to his lips. 'We don't want them to know we're following them.'

Quietly as they could, they followed the line of soldiers to the field at the end of the village.

'I think their heading for the electricity pylon,' whispered Hobo.

'Look!' Lucy bent down and picked up one of the soldiers' parachutes. 'It has a message on it.'

Hobo pushed Lucy aside, shining his torch on the flimsy plastic.

'Oi! I'm here, you know.'

'It's tiny writing,' he said, ignoring her.

'It says, "Mission abort. Reconvene at the pylon at twenty-two hundred hours to be picked up".'

'See, they are aliens,' Lucy breathed. I was beginning to think I'd gone mad.'

'But why hide themselves in crackers?' Hobo rubbed his head. 'It doesn't make any sense.'

A shower of sparks lit up the night sky. One of the soldiers began to fire its tiny gun at the cable at the top of the pylon.

'I think they're trying to knock out the electricity,' Lucy said, just as all the street lights went out.

'The little blighters,' said Hobo.

'Blighters,' said Lucy. 'How old are you?'

'Saw it in a war film!'

More of the soldiers made it to the top.

Lucy grabbed a handful of snow and threw it at the pylon. 'Take that,' she roared.

Hobo quickly followed suit, throwing one after the other, his arms spinning like sails on a windmill.

'Harder!' yelled Lucy as she gathered handfuls of snow, quickly turning them into ice balls.

Copying Hobo's windmill-like action, she started hurling snowballs with all her strength at the strange plastic invaders.

Hobo stopped suddenly, and stared in amazement, his jaw dropping like a stone down a well. Some of the plastic soldiers had deployed their parachutes and were gently being carried away on the breeze. An intense yellow light filled the sky and the plastic soldiers disappeared. All of them, carried away into the void.

'What just happened? Where did they go?' Lucy shouted as she gazed into the inky black sky.

'Obviously back to their ship,' said Hobo. 'Just like the note said.'

'Well, good riddance to them.' Lucy rubbed the top of her arms.

Hobo walked towards the pylon. 'I'm just going to check around the base. Make sure they have all gone.'

As they turned for home, the streetlights all popped back on, one after another.

Back at Lucy's house Lucy and Hobo tore open the last

remaining crackers and all the boxes were empty.

'They've all gone,' Hobo said. 'But where?'

'No idea, but I think we're safe now.'

In the warm kitchen, Hobo shook the snow off his coat like a dog caught in the rain.

'Hey!' Lucy jumped back. 'You're soaking me.'

'You were already wet.' Hobo gave her a cheeky grin.

Lucy flung her coat over the chair and they went to join her parents on the sofa.

'Where have you two been?' asked Dad

'Just having fun in the snow,' said Lucy. She winked at Hobo.

'Your mum and I couldn't resist pulling a cracker each,' said Dad.

Lucy and Hobo exchanged worried looks.

'What was in them?' asked Lucy nervously.

'I got a spinning top,' said Mum.

'And I got a nail file,' laughed Dad. 'We saved one for each of you,' he held them out.

'I think we'll keep these for Christmas Day.' Lucy shook the crackers firmly before shoving them down the sofa. 'Just in case they go off unexpectedly,' she said.

'You two are bonkers,' said Dad. He couldn't for the life of him work out why she and Hobo dissolved into fits of laughter.

THE CHRISTMAS CRACKER CONUNDRUM!

Tim Gambrell

It was the morning of the last day of term. The Christmas holidays beckoned. Lucy Wilson, along with her tutor group, filed into the school hall. Years 7, 8 and 9 were being treated to a touring pantomime that morning. Hobo Kostinen would be in among the throng somewhere, too. The banner across the stage read 'The Big Bang Theatre Company'. The actors were standing there already. Only three of them. And they were going to perform *Aladdin*. Lucy thought of all the characters in the Disney film and wondered how they'd ever manage it. She wasn't the only one with a cynical attitude towards this 'kids' stuff'. But, as others pointed out, it was time out of lessons and that couldn't be bad.

Lucy was surprised to find herself enjoying the show almost from the off. The actors played many characters each and there was plenty of slapstick comedy. Most of the actual jokes were truly awful puns, and the actors tended to groan at them along with the audience. Lucy could see some of the teachers having a 'right old time of it', laughing away.

At the end of the show, the Genie, Aladdin and Princess Jasmine all came together for a bow. The crowd, despite its early cynicism, clapped like mad. Lucy wore a huge grin. Two seats away, Mel was pumping her fist and doing annoying whooping. The three actors each produced a Christmas cracker.

'That's where they got the jokes from,' muttered

Lucy in a semi-whisper. Nearby chuckles suggested some of her class agreed. The actors then came together, a cracker end in each hand, and began to walk around in a circle. They spun faster and faster, the audience loving the suspense, waiting for one of the crackers to go off.

All three crackers went off in one huge bang and flash, like fireworks. *They must have been special stage crackers*, Lucy thought afterwards. No ordinary crackers went off with that kind of power. The whole school cheered and applauded harder than ever. As the smoke cleared from the stage, there was no sign of the three actors, their banner, props or costumes. The theatre company had literally vanished. Proper magic!

What was certain through the chatter was that lessons were a waste of time. Everyone wanted the Big Bang Theatre Company to return again sometime.

The following day, Saturday, was one of those family days where Lucy and her mum just seemed to be on different wavelengths the whole time. Conall, Dean and Hannah were coming to stay for Christmas. They usually spent Christmas Day with Dean's family, and Mum had always struggled to hide her disappointment. Now that Lucy, Mum and Dad had moved from London to Ogmore-by-Sea, things were changing, it seemed. Con, Dean and Hannah were arriving the following day, and Mum was determined to make everything 'just right' as she termed it. As a consequence, she was spending all her time hassling Lucy and Dad. They kept being told to clean this, that and the other. All the while, Mum made lists and schedules, and checked whether they had enough tubs of Celebrations.

It would all be worth it, though. Lucy loved Con and Dean to bits, and little Hannah, their adopted daughter, was such a gorgeous little bundle of fun. Having them there would make Christmas vastly more bearable in Lucy's view. Plus, Con always got her awesome presents. And she knew it wasn't supposed to be about 'receiving gifts' as Mum and Dad loved to remind her. But, still – you know. An awesome present made for an awesome Christmas, that's the way it was!

Lucy and Dad were sneaking a quick drink and a biscuit in the kitchen. This was a good day for the two of *them*, for a change. They'd come together in adversity, thanks to Mum's obsessiveness.

'Careful to eat it over the sink,' Dad said as he handed her the open biscuit barrel. 'You know Mum'll spot the crumbs on the floor.'

It was at this moment that Lucy's phone beeped. She was so pleased they were using their phones again. It was a text from Hobo:

Seafront. Now. *Gotta see this!*

BRT, Lucy quickly replied. She downed the rest of her juice, then headed to the porch for her Ugg boots and Parka. It was too cold down at the front for her usual hoodie and Converse. Dad peered round the kitchen door and raised his eyebrows. Lucy shrugged an apology for leaving him in the lurch.

'Mum?' she yelled. 'Just gotta pop out and help Hobo with something.'

Dad tucked back into the kitchen. He didn't have a great deal of time for her best friend. There was a pause, then Mum's feet thundered out of the spare bedroom and down the stairs.

'This had better be important, Lucy.'

'It is, Mum, honest.'

Mum glared at her, intently. 'All right then, but don't be long. We've only got today to get this place in order.'

'Mum, it's already immaculate.'

'There's plenty more to do yet, young lady. You be back in good time for lunch.'

She said she'd do just that, then slipped quickly out through the door. As it closed behind her she heard Mum say, 'Albert, are those biscuit crumbs on the floor?'

It was an overcast day, but there was still snow on

the ground. In London, at that time of the year, this would have made it a warm winter day. A hoodie day. Here, in Ogmore, there was the perpetual sea breeze. On a truly cold day it could freeze the tears at the corners of your eyes and numb your nose. It wasn't quite that bad today, but Lucy was glad to be wrapped in her Parka at least.

She could tell from a distance that something was up at the seafront. Usually, at this time of the year, apart from the odd dog-walker, the car park next to the seafront was empty save for the tacky old Christmas lights which adorned the perimeter fence, the public toilets and the telephone booth – which smelled like a toilet. The lights seemed, to Lucy, to be tired leftovers from the 1950s, or whenever Ogmore-by-Sea was a popular seaside resort. But this morning there was a mass of kids there too. Kids from her school, she noted. Hobo stood apart from the main group. He waved to her as she approached. She saw that he was holding something. It was a Christmas cracker.

'Come see, come see,' Hobo said.

Lucy made her way through the crowd. In the centre, with the sea as a backdrop, was a sort of pop-up promotional stand. Four girls stood around it, handing out a free Christmas cracker to each child. Just one each, Lucy noted. The girls were strikingly beautiful – flawless, almost like life-size dolls. Each wore a kind of Santa Claus dress and black boots. One of the girls, a brunette, handed a cracker to Lucy.

'Remember,' the girl said as she placed a cracker in Lucy's hand. 'It's a special one, just for you. Keep it for Christmas Day.' She smiled at Lucy, then blinked. As she did so, Lucy was momentarily convinced the girl's pupils disappeared, just leaving the milky eyeball. But when she looked again the eyes were fine. The girl quickly looked away to see if anyone else wanted a cracker. Lucy figured she'd just been dazzled by a reflection from the sea.

'Thanks for the heads-up,' said Lucy as she joined Hobo again, looking the cracker over.

'I hope these don't contain plastic soldiers.' He gave her a momentary smile.

'I doubt it,' said Lucy with a shrug.

'You're a bit off the boil today,' said Hobo.

'Yeah, sorry. Mum's been all uptight about Christmas. She's had me and Dad up since early doors, working us into the ground.'

'Did you see the branding?'

Lucy looked at her cracker, then back at the stall. The area around it had cleared a bit, now that the kids had accepted that they'd only be given one cracker each. *Big Bang Crackers*, she read to herself. It rang a bell from somewhere.

'Of course!' Lucy burst. 'The same name as that theatre company.' Hobo gave her a thumbs up. The stand's banner claimed that there was *a surprise in every cracker, and it's out of this world!* 'Could just be marketing speak, I guess.' She looked at Hobo somewhat hopefully. Couldn't they have a quiet Christmas?

'But their eyes,' he said, and Lucy knew she hadn't imagined it.

Crackers had been handed out to all the kids. The greedy ones, pushing for a second, had been skillfully sent on their way. The pretty cracker girls then came together around the pop-up stand. Lucy noticed that this was like the end of the pantomime at school and started to back away, pulling Hobo with her. The girls linked hands, via a Big Bang Christmas cracker each, and then leaned outwards. The tug as they leaned back was enough to pull their crackers. There was a huge explosion of light and sound, which knocked all the kids in the vicinity to the ground – Lucy and Hobo included. When they picked themselves up again, they found that the pop-up stand and the girls had all vanished.

'More magic,' muttered Hobo.

The rest of the kids were thrilled and amazed, like they had been at the end of *Aladdin*. They wowed and whooped and cheered, even though the stand and the girls had gone.

'Yeah,' agreed Lucy. 'And this time I don't buy

it at all.'

Children rarely follow instructions when unsupervised. Once the Big Bang stand had disappeared, the crowd of kids all started to pull their crackers, eager to find their 'out of this world' surprise. Lucy and Hobo, being already suspicious about the crackers, held on to theirs. But Lucy knew that, even if they hadn't already been suspicious, the puffs of green smoke emitted with every big bang would have been more than enough to make her and Hobo pause.

The bang seemed to be it, though. No paper hat, no awful jokes, no trinkets as far as they could see. Just the very loud bang and the green smoke – which dispersed quickly on the sea breeze. The cracker halves were being discarded on the ground. Lucy was having none of that.

'Oi! You lot, pick up your rubbish!'

A few of the kids closest by looked her way. Their faces were glazed over, as if they'd been hypnotized. Lucy shuddered as she saw their eyeballs momentarily disappear in a haze of green, before returning. Then the children seemed to switch back to normal and headed straight off, presumably back to their homes. No one was complaining about the lack of toy or joke or paper hat. In fact, it seemed like they'd all completely forgotten about the crackers. Lucy tried in vain to get some of her classmates, at least, to pick up their discarded remains. It was like they all had an inability to see what she could see.

Once left on their own, Lucy and Hobo both had the same thought. They bent to examine some of the cracker remains. Whatever they were, they certainly weren't traditional Christmas crackers. Beneath the shiny cardboard exterior was some sort of sealed container (not quite plastic, not quite metal, according to Hobo). The containers had all split along the middle and separated. Presumably this was what produced the loud bang. There was no sign of the usual cracker 'fuse' anyway. Lucy looked at the unused cracker she still held. The bulging middle section was certainly sealed; there was no way in from either end. She was careful not to do anything that might accidentally set it off.

A waxy residue remained on the inside of the used crackers. *This is probably from the smoke*, Lucy thought. It certainly smelled nasty when they were up close like that. After touching it, both Lucy and Hobo found their fingertips became irritated and had to swill them in a puddle. Not a safe substance, then.

'Lucky they were pulled out here in the open air,' said Hobo. 'I reckon that smoke could have done serious damage if the crackers were used in a packed family dining room.'

'You think it could kill the person?'

Hobo shrugged. 'It's certainly more like a grenade than a Christmas cracker, don't you reckon?'

'Big bang. It said so on the banner.'

'Yeah,' he agreed. 'Merry booming Christmas.'

'So, what do we do with this lot? Report it to the council as hazardous waste?'

A rustling, crumpling sound made them look again at the cracker remains. As they watched, each piece curled up, folded in on itself and reduced down to nothing. It was like watching clingfilm held over a Bunsen burner. Something about the materials must have reacted with the air, causing a fast decay and dispersal. Before they knew it, nothing remained.

No sooner had the cracker remains dissolved away to nothing, than Lucy's phone started ringing.

'Mum,' she sighed, looking at the flashing screen. Lucy answered the call and was immediately subjected to a tirade about being out enjoying herself when there were mince pies to be made and presents still to wrap. She held the phone at arm's length to let Hobo share in her seasonal joy.

'Mum? MUM?' she yelled. 'Breathe!' The voice halted. 'I'm heading home now, don't worry.' Lucy hung up. 'Christmas,' she grumbled. 'What a load of hard work.' She smiled at Hobo and indicated where the crackers had been. 'What are we gonna do about all this lot?'

Hobo shrugged. 'Let's keep our ones safe somewhere. Don't let them get pulled, whatever we do. I guess we'll just have to keep an eye out for anything suspicious with the rest of the kids. That whole eye thing could just be nothing, I suppose.'

He didn't sound very convinced, and Lucy gave him a look which told him that she wasn't either.

'Eyes open, ears open, mouth shut. Standard procedure – Lethbridge-Stewart stuff.'

They nodded firmly to one another, then went their separate ways.

Whatever else was going on in the world, the remainder of that day passed uneventfully in Ogmore-by-Sea. Hobo was much less restricted than Lucy, owing to his family being a lot more chilled out and his mum having to put in extra hours on duty to cover Christmas leave of the regular police officers. Hobo texted Lucy a lot of updates at first – which were, basically, 'nothing to report'. She was stuck listening to *Now That's What I Call Christmas* on repeat, while polishing glasses, wrapping presents and writing last minute cards for the neighbours. She wasn't allowed to deliver the cards, though. She could tell Mum didn't trust her not to nip off once she was outside.

Lucy tried to get her own back when decorating

the Christmas cake with Dad. She was cutting out fondant shapes and he wasn't paying that much attention, so she mixed in a few Halloween bats and brooms for a laugh. Then Mum came in to check halfway and Lucy felt bad for getting Dad into trouble.

Before Lucy knew it, it was Sunday: Christmas Eve. Conall, Dean and Hannah arrived in time for a late lunch and the house was filled with mirth and drinks and food, not to mention the squeals of little Hannah as she investigated her grandparents' house. It made Lucy think about Grandad. She'd been a little older than Hannah when she'd got to know him, but visiting Grandad had always held that same sense of thrill and wonder.

The visiting Londoners were charmed by Ogmore's rugged beauty. Mid-afternoon, they all went for a walk to the seafront. Conall stayed behind to prepare his special chilli for dinner, much better than Mum's, he said. Lucy wanted to stay behind at first, but then she realised this was her first chance since Saturday to see what was going on in the village, so she went along instead.

She sent Hobo a text telling him what she was up to. On returning home, all she could do was repeat what he'd previously texted her: nothing to report. There'd been a few kids out and about that she recognised from school, but always with parents in tow, and none of them acting suspiciously in any way. She even started to wonder if Hobo's throwaway comment had been right after all? Maybe the whole thing *was* just nothing.

Christmas Day was little Hannah's day, really. Lucy was relieved. It took all the pressure off her. She was no longer the youngest in the family, no longer the focus of everyone's attention. She found she could relax and enjoy herself a lot more – which was exactly what she needed. Con and Dean had given her an extremely long multi-coloured scarf, and a new simulated world computer game, and she was even able to escape to her bedroom for a bit, to install it onto her laptop. She'd been waiting for that since February, even though it had only been out since June. She gave them both an extra special hug.

After a lazy breakfast, the phone calls began. Grandpa Sam, Nick, Kate, Cousin Gordon, and even a call from cousins in Africa. All to wish everyone a Happy Christmas. All to be passed from person to person for an individual chat. Except Grandpa Sam; he just spoke to Mum and then had to go. By the time they'd opened the rest of the presents, cleared away the wrapping paper and sat down to eat, Christmas lunch had become Christmas dinner. Poor Hannah fell asleep over her pudding. Dean popped her upstairs to Lucy's room, where they'd set up the travel cot, and Lucy went up with her too. She appreciated a bit of quiet time, and she'd watch over Hannah while she played her new game for a bit.

Lucy knew she'd done the right thing. She felt happy and contented, and the sounds filtering up from downstairs suggested the grown-ups were appreciating being able to let their hair down a bit more. Her mood was interrupted by the telephone ringing. After a few rings it was clear that they couldn't hear it over the music and laughter downstairs. Lucy dashed out onto the landing, where the other handset sat on a table. It was Hobo.

'Merry Christmas!'

Lucy responded in a harsh whisper. 'You might have woken Hannah!'

'Sorry,' he replied, 'I didn't know.'

This was true, and Lucy realised she was being unfair.

'No, no, I'm sorry. Merry Christmas, Hobo. What's up? How's your day?'

'It's the kids with the crackers,' he said, not really answering her question. 'As far as I can see, they're all returning to the seafront. Now.'

Before Lucy could even respond, there was a huge bang from downstairs. With alarm, Lucy realised she didn't have a clue where her Big Bang cracker had ended up. She hoped to goodness that wasn't it being pulled downstairs.

'Lucy, you okay?'

'Gotta go, Hobo. I'll join you on the seafront, soon as.'

The noise had woken Hannah. Lucy scooped her up and dashed downstairs. Bursting into the living room, she was greeted by a foul smell and the faint vestiges of green smoke. Conall, Dean and Mum were lying unconscious across the easy chair and sofa. There was no sign of Dad. Trying not to panic, she placed Hannah between Con and Dean on the sofa then rushed to the front bay windows and threw them open. Immediately the room was filled with the fresh chill of the sea air. She threw open the patio doors to try to create a through-draught.

Frantically she gave Mum, then Dean, then Conall a rough shake to try to wake them. They were breathing at least. Conall came-to first, coughing and spluttering, but aware enough to know that his daughter needed comforting next to him. Lucy quickly ran them each a big glass of water. Conall downed his immediately, then set to rousing Dean.

Dean groggily opened his eyes. 'What happened?' He shivered with the cold.

'Did Dad have a special cracker?' Lucy asked, trying not to sound frantic.

Conall nodded. 'He found it in the box. After you went upstairs, Mum realised none had been set for the meal.'

'Right,' Lucy replied, grabbing her hoodie from the back of the dining chair where she'd left it earlier. 'You stay here and make sure Mum's okay. Leave Dad to me.'

Lucy was immediately struck by how dark it was outside. It was past sundown anyway, but this felt different. This was darker than normal, and in the distance Lucy could see the washed-out coloured lights along the seafront. As her eyes adjusted she spotted the large group of children gathered there, and to one side of the group was a taller figure, clearly her dad, silhouetted against the backdrop of the sea. She rushed off after him.

Instinct made Lucy cautious. As she approached the seafront she didn't call out to Dad. She kept within shaded areas where possible and crept the last hundred metres or so. She couldn't see Hobo anywhere and he hadn't answered her text asking where he was. Suddenly, a hand clamped over her mouth and she found herself tugged backwards into the deeper shadows.

Lucy spun around and shoved her attacker away. Hobo staggered back into the wall and an old dustbin clattered under him. His hands shot up in panic and Lucy looked back towards Dad and the group of children. There was no visible reaction.

'Sorry,' Hobo said. 'I guess I panicked a bit.'

'Next time try hissing at me, or just replying to my text.'

'Battery's dead,' he replied. 'That bang, when I phoned you. I take it your dad pulled the cracker?'

Lucy nodded.

'I saw him. He looks possessed, just like all the others. And they've all reverted to how they were just after the crackers exploded on Saturday. Why's it so dark tonight? Thick cloud?'

'Dunno, too dark to see.'

'Hang on.' Lucy looked upwards, gripped by a thought. 'We can't see any stars, but even on the darkest nights you can see if there's a blanket of cloud above. And there is, out at sea. But up above us here it's like—'

'Like something's floating there, blotting out the sky.'

With a hum of electricity, the whole area was suddenly brightly floodlit. From the pattern of the lights as they beamed down, Lucy could tell there was some sort of flying saucer hovering a few hundred metres above them. The beams were lighting her dad and the children, who were all looking up, raising their hands expectantly as if to a parent, requesting to be picked up. What was this? Alien abduction? She looked at Hobo and chewed her lip.

'We've got to do something before they all get abducted.'

Hobo pulled his Big Bang cracker from his inside pocket. 'Worth the risk, you reckon? Get one of us on the inside?'

'But what if there's no way back?'

'Then that means you've lost your dad. Lucy, we've got to try.'

Lucy grudgingly agreed and promised Hobo she'd do all she could to keep him as much himself. He grasped the cracker with both hands and pulled it apart.

The bang, that close, was tremendous. But still the others on the promenade didn't look their way.

'Hobo?'

His face was rapt. His eyes had turned milky white all over, but his pupils didn't reappear like those of the other children had. This was different.

'Hobo,' Lucy repeated. 'Are you still there?'

He opened his mouth. 'There is resistance.' It was his voice, but clearly not his own words. 'Why am I not totally absorbed?'

Lucy only now noticed a bulge on Hobo's upper forehead, something throbbing just under the skin. It had a faint greenish tint, visible through Hobo's hairless head in the bright lights from the spaceship above. Was this what the cracker had contained? An alien mind parasite? Out of this world, indeed. Lucy felt her stomach turn, but she managed to hold things together.

'Who are you? What are you? And why have you come here?'

'We have never found the need to name ourselves. But humans would understand us best as protist nemavores – amoeba. We have come here because we need human children.'

'Lucy?' This was Hobo struggling against the thing that was trying to control his mind and take over his body. 'I can feel the alien in my mind, see their plans.'

'It said they need human children, Hobo. What for?'

'Host bodies.' He was clearly struggling and the lump on his skull was pulsating angrily. 'Refresh the gene stock in their matter manipulator.'

Hobo's posture changed as the creature took back control. 'Our hosts need to be willing. Children can be more easily manipulated. And they last longer.'

'You have my dad, too.'

Hobo's face sagged. Lucy wasn't sure what was happening. Then her friend's body spoke again.

'I have sensed him. Our leader, no less. Mature humanoids do not often succumb. He must have been unusually susceptible.'

'Half a bottle of wine, I expect,' mumbled Lucy

to herself.

'However, the body is unlikely to provide much support and longevity. He will be disposed of once we are back on board our ship.' Hobo turned and walked over to join the rest of the crowd in the light.

Lucy was appalled. She followed Hobo. She knew she had to act fast to save everyone. But what could she do?

With a hazy green glow, the pantomime actors and cracker girls reappeared on the seafront. Even from some distance away, Lucy could see that this time they all looked sickly and diseased. The green glow spread out towards the gathered children. Dad strode over to the decrepit arrivals. She could see him drawing deep breaths within the gaseous glow as he went.

'Come,' he called to the others. 'Breathe in the fumes. We must complete the conversion before transfer.'

Lucy watched, frantically hoping inspiration would strike. There was no way of knowing if the conversion would be reversible. If it wasn't, then Hobo, Dad and all the kids couldn't be rescued. Dad started to speak again, this time to the diseased figures.

'You creatures are near termination. The gene pool has been over-stretched. You have delivered your final service, our new genetic source.' The synthetic bodies reached out a pleading hand, then seemed to just flake away like withered leaves on the sea breeze.

Dad turned and gestured to everyone. For the first time since she got to the seafront, she saw his face. She nearly screamed. There was a large green blob on his forehead – the amoeba leader, according to Hobo. This one hadn't even made it under the skin. But Dad's face showed he was completely under its control.

Lucy started to cough. The mist was slowly getting thicker and she had to back away to keep out of its reach. She pulled her hood up, to try to use it like a face mask, but there was something inside it stopping her. She reached back and pulled out... a Christmas cracker! An ordinary one. She bet that was Conall, playing a trick on her. But now she had it, could it be any use? *Depends what's inside it*, she thought.

She grabbed an end in each hand and pulled. As she did so, she stepped into a divot on the grass and stumbled backwards. The cracker went off with its usual bang. But Lucy hadn't considered that the green gas might be flammable. The spark from her cracker was enough and suddenly, from her vantage point on the ground, she saw the whole green cloud disappear, with a whoosh of orange flame.

There was a terrible scream from Dad. Lucy was immediately on her feet again and rushing towards him. He was lying, prone, on the ground. She felt for a pulse. He was still alive. All the kids had also collapsed. Lucy hoped to goodness that none of them had been hurt by the flames. The green jelly from Dad's forehead was now lying on the ground to one side. It was crispy and dry, like seaweed from a sushi meal. It was still moving, though, and Lucy could hear a plaintive cry in the back of her mind, claiming that without the gas they would all die. Lucy bent to pick the large amoeba up and immediately felt its presence more strongly in her head.

'You,' it told her. 'Yes, you will do much better. Prepare to be absorbed into our genetic manipulator.'

'I don't think so,' she told it. 'You're dealing with a Lethbridge-Stewart, here. Protector of the Earth.'

Her Christmas cracker had contained a set of nail clippers, and Lucy prodded and nipped at the crispy edge of the jelly with them.

With a few 'oohs' and 'aahs', the amoeboid leader begged for clemency.

'We underestimated the intelligence and adaptability of human children,' it said. Lucy wasn't entirely surprised why, when the leader revealed the source of its information. Much of what they assumed about humanity was based on what they believed were broadcasts by the human leader. Lucy pointed out that the president of the United States was only one human leader, but he tended to shout the loudest.

'I don't understand,' she asked. 'Why do you just need children?'

'We cannot do much, physically, for ourselves, Lucy Wilson. We are amoeboid. Our technology is borrowed. The spaceship you see above was found discarded on our home world. Its operation is based around the standard humanoid form. The spaceship contains a matter manipulator, and our amoeboid forms were able to take over the new bodies it created. But quickly they started to die. We realised that the unit depends on a regular update of the genetic pattern. We have periodically roamed the galaxy since, to search out suitable new species. Children work better for our needs than adults. The gene pool stays fresher longer.'

Lucy's next question seemed obvious to her, but she was surprised by the response.

'Why don't you build robots instead?'

'I do not understand, Lucy Wilson. What are *robots*?'

Hobo staggered over to join Lucy, his amoeba now quivering on the outside of his head, clearly struggling to hold on.

'Hobo, you okay?'

He nodded. His eyeballs had returned to normal. 'I could hear your conversation in my head. I suspect we all could. I like your suggestion, but I'm thinking if their technology is borrowed and the ship didn't contain any robots, then that's why they don't understand the concept.'

'They're only clever enough to use what they've got, not extend the concepts?'

'Seems likely,' Hobo agreed.

The voice returned to her head. 'Help us, Lucy Wilson, please?'

Lucy looked sternly at the crispy amoeba in her hand. 'You see,' she said. 'That's all you needed to say in the first place.'

The interior of the spaceship was everything the jelly amoeba creatures weren't. It was dull, grey, hard and sharp. A few humanoid 'hosts' remained at the control posts. Lucy could see that it wasn't very comfortable for them to live in and operate, even though it was designed for them. The bridge had been temporarily vented of the green gas and filled with air instead, to allow Lucy and Hobo to breathe. Hobo's 'host' had now left him.

To one side of the bridge was the matter manipulator. It looked like a large vat or tank, filled with gloop; a series of booths were connected to it via rubber tubes. Like the rest of what they'd seen, it was purely functional. There was no beauty or art to any of it. Lucy was convinced this ship must have originated from some aggressive, warlike species. She hoped she'd never get to meet them, whoever they were.

Lucy placed the leader in its ceremonial bowl, as directed. There it could breathe the gas again, and its injuries would heal. She watched it as it frolicked happily. Then it spoke.

'Show me these robots.'

'The rest of the children, and my dad, will be released, unharmed?'

'You have my word as leader, Lucy Wilson.'

Lucy pulled out her phone. She still had 4G. Nice. She opened the YouTube app and pulled up some videos of real and fictional robots in operation.

'We will transfer images from the device onto our main screen,' said the leader. Lucy selected a video. The image on the ship's main screen showed the seashore below, with all the bodies still lying unconscious. As Lucy played the video the screen image changed to YouTube.

After several videos, the leader asked Lucy to stop. The screen changed again. Blueprints appeared there. Robot design and construction information.

'Yes,' it said. 'I believe we can construct one of these.'

Hobo pointed out that the leader's gas-filled

globe would sit securely on the shoulders of the robot, like a head. And then afterwards they could get the robot to make more like it.

'You just let them keep going until you have all you need,' Hobo said, with a grin. Lucy hoped that wouldn't amount to an army, but she kept her fears to herself.

'Thank you, both of you. We have a way forward.'

'Season of goodwill, and all that,' quipped Hobo. He'd barely got the words out when the two friends found themselves beamed back to the seafront below.

Lucy and Hobo immediately looked up, but the spaceship had already gone. There above them once again was the night sky. All around them the children of Ogmore started waking, shocked and frightened – unaware of what they were doing on the seafront and clearly themselves once again. The area was then invaded by concerned parents and relatives. Thankfully, no one was looking for answers, only to find their wandering children.

Lucy spotted Dad and rushed to help him up. He was very woozy.

'Dad? You okay?'

'Mr Wilson, Albert? It's Hobo. Can you hear me?'

'Wuh?' Dad blinked at them both, blearily.

Lucy had an idea. 'No father can resist these at Christmas.' She smiled at Hobo's confusion, as she found the cracker joke in her trouser pocket. 'Here's one for you, Dad. Why was Santa's helper depressed? He had low elf-esteem!'

Dad responded to the awful pun, groggily muttering that he must remember that one for the office.

'I'm glad I don't work where he works,' said Hobo. Lucy grinned at both of them, then placed the paper hat from her cracker on Dad's head.

'What am I doing down at the front?' he asked, rapidly becoming more lucid. 'It's freezing. Why would I come out without a coat on?'

'We found you down here, Dad.'

'Blimey. Mum's gonna kill me. I'm not drinking again this Christmas.'

Lucy and Hobo guided him homewards. A knowing glance passed between them as Dad started to hum *A Spaceman Came Travelling*. They smiled and joined in.

CRIMES OF FASHION

Terry Cooper

As the sun came up on Ogmore-by-Sea, the waves rolled gently onto the shore, trying their best not to make too much noise.

The empty seafront was interrupted by a sole figure. Alwyn Ashford was training for a local 10K race that was coming up in the New Year, and he had made it his mission to be up at the crack of dawn to get a mile or two on the road before work.

He had the motivation, the fitness gear, new running shoes and was feeling fitter by the day. He felt like he was ready for anything, that nothing could take him by surprise. Then suddenly he found himself enclosed in a blinding yellow light and disappeared without trace... That definitely came as a surprise.

The following evening a local teenager, Andy Shackleton, and his girlfriend Laura were walking home from a particularly exhausting but fun game of tennis. Before they reached their destination, they too were taken away by the bright yellow light.

The same night, Russ Price, the town's local boxing champ, staggered out of his local pub, feeling a little ill. He shivered as the cold night air hit him, and he remembered that his expensive new coat had a cool feature. He pressed a small button on the cuff, and the jacket warmed up from the inside. Nice and toasty. It was an expensive purchase, but worth every penny. Russ pulled out his mobile phone and dialled for a taxi to take him home. But the phone didn't work. The screen was flickering and he couldn't hear anything except a high-pitched buzzing. Then he disappeared. Swallowed up by an intense yellow light!

Lucy Wilson sat up in bed and yawned. She was starting to go stir crazy. She'd enjoyed the last few days of festive activities at home – the presents, party games, seemingly endless stream of visitors, the must-see Christmas telly and more food than she could ever remember eating before. Oh, and, of course, going to a spaceship and meeting jelly amoeba creatures, but that was par for the course for Lucy Wilson, space adventurer!

But now all of that had subsided, and things had become a little quieter around the house. She was looking forward to seeing the outside world again, no matter how cold it might be out there.

Anyway, she'd got a thick woolly bobble hat for Christmas from Mum, and a very, very long stripy scarf from Conall and Dean. Armed with the hat and scarf, she felt more than ready to take on the elements. All she needed was for Hobo to break her out.

Salvation came in the form of a text from Hobo that afternoon. From the sound of the text, her friend was climbing the walls and itching to get out too.

Lucy was dressed and out of the house in record time.

Hobo was walking towards the café when Lucy came bounding along. 'Whoa! Take it easy!' called Hobo when he saw her.

'What are you on about?' asked Lucy.

Hobo indicated the woollen python around her neck. 'That thing's so long, I thought you were going to trip yourself up on it. Didn't they have one in your size?'

'Hah! I love it actually,' said Lucy, wrapping another three feet of it around her neck to keep it off the floor. 'It's super handy. Whoever knitted it must've had too much time on their hands.'

'Or too much wool and didn't know when to stop?' said Hobo. 'Let me guess, a Christmas present from a crazy long-lost auntie?' he asked.

'Nope,' said Lucy. 'Conall gave it to me. He told me it was a family heirloom, handed down from Grandad. So it's kind of special. But don't ask me where Grandad got it from. He wasn't exactly the type to wear a crazy, impractical thing like this!'

Hobo rubbed his hands together, trying to keep them warm. He nodded in the direction of the café, which was heated, and had an unoccupied table near the window.

'Let's get a cuppa? It's positively hypothermic

out here!'

'That's not a proper word!' laughed Lucy. Hobo smiled.

'It is,' he said, opening the café door, 'Indubitably!'

Once they had started on their extra-large mugs of hot chocolate, Lucy and Hobo compared Christmases. Lucy had more actual gifts, but Hobo received more money.

'So what are you going to splash out on first?' asked Lucy, warming her hands on the mug.

Hobo looked around the café as he answered. 'I don't know really.'

'What about the sports gear that everybody's wearing?' asked Lucy.

'It's not really my scene,' replied Hobo.

'I think it's funky, in a weird kind of way.' Lucy indicated a small group of teenagers nearby. They were wearing flashy jackets in a shiny, multi-coloured material. It looked sort of pearl and seemed to change colour depending on how it moved in the light. Others had matching trainers, and one girl had a backpack in the same style.

'Looks expensive,' said Hobo, shrugging.

'Yes, I guess it's a bit sporty for you.'

'Not really. I mean, I don't play football, but I can run pretty fast when I need to. Almost as fast as you!'

'Yeah, almost,' said Lucy. 'Your long legs and arms help.'

'I'm super aerodynamic too,' added Hobo, pointing to his hairless head.

Lucy smiled. 'Do you feel the cold up there? You must do. I've got too much hair and you've got none.'

Hobo nodded. 'Actually, I can't remember what it's like to have hair. So I guess I'm used to it. But if I get too cold, can I use your scarf as a turban? That'll do the trick!'

Both of them laughed. Lucy's smile faded when she realised there was no more hot chocolate left in her mug.

'So, you want to go and spend some of that fortune you've got saved up, then?' she asked. 'How about some window shopping?'

'Sounds like a plan,' agreed Hobo, finishing the last of his drink. 'Although we have plenty of windows at home.'

'Not funny, Hobo.'

Just as they were about to leave, Hobo caught a glimpse of the telly in the corner of the café. The local news was mentioning the disappearance of a number of villagers in the last few days.

'Wait a minute. I know that man!' said Hobo.

'Which man?' asked Lucy.

'Alwyn Ashford. He's a runner. Not as fast as you, more like long distance running.'

'You think he got lost?' asked Lucy. 'Or something worse? Kidnapped?'

Hobo stared at the screen. 'They don't say. But look – another missing person is that boxer, Russ Price. He's hard as nails. I can't see him getting kidnapped by anyone – he'd knock 'em out!'

'You might be right,' said Lucy. 'Maybe they just went to London or somewhere for Christmas and forgot to tell anyone? I dunno. Could be anything, but I hope it's nothing bad.'

'Hmm, yeah. I'd hate to get lost in the city,' said Hobo.

After a few minutes of window shopping and no purchases, Lucy and Hobo found themselves standing outside Protheroe's Surf Shack. It wasn't a shack as such, but it was a shop that sold mostly surfboards, fishing rods and diving equipment. It did well in the summer when there were plenty of tourists looking to enjoy the sea.

'Hey, this place sells that sportswear you like – look!' said Hobo.

The window was decorated with the shiny jackets, shoes and bags, all glistening and colourful. Lucy's eyes were wide with temptation.

'Ooh! Look at it, Hobo!' she said, touching the cold window. 'I could see myself in one of those jackets. They look pretty sweet, don't they?'

Hobo scrunched his nose up. 'Well, it's not really my thing, but if you want one, let's pop in and check them out.'

'They're not open in the winter,' said Lucy.

Hobo pushed the door and it opened. 'Well, they are today! Come on!' she said.

Mr Protheroe was pottering about in his shop when he saw Lucy and Hobo come in. He put a large crate on the floor and smiled at his customers.

'Hiya kids! Had a good Christmas?'

'Yes thanks,' said Hobo.

Lucy wandered around the shop, her long scarf trailing behind her.

'Nice scarf,' said Mr Protheroe.

Lucy smiled, almost embarrassed by the compliment.

Mr Protheroe turned to face Hobo. 'You're Megan's boy, aren't you? I know your mother! She was a big help when I had a break-in at the shop.'

'I thought you were closed in December?' asked Hobo.

'I am, normally. But I've got a new line in, see?' He pointed to the funky clothing all around the shop. 'It's selling like hot cakes at the moment. I'd be mad not to open up this week.'

Lucy and her long scarf continued to explore the shop. Some crates were stacked up by the wall. Lucy noticed that one was wet, and had sand on it. A thin sliver of seaweed was trapped between it and the crate underneath, which was also wet and sandy.

'All the rage it is,' said Mr Protheroe, picking up the crate from the floor and placing it on the counter. 'Cracking quality too. Have a look.'

Hobo and Lucy went to the counter, where Mr Protheroe opened the crate, and pulled out a large coat.

'Try this on, buddy! You look like a man of taste.'

Hobo put it on, and it was a good fit. It had comfortable sleeves, plenty of pockets and a smooth surface, a bit like a wetsuit. Hobo squirmed. It wasn't his usual thing, but he did quite like it.

'Looks good,' said Lucy.

'You think?' asked Hobo. 'You're not just saying that?'

'Course not. But can you afford it? That's the question.'

Mr Protheroe pointed at the jacket proudly.

'Eighty-five quid, those are. Bargain! Not many left! Get it while they're in stock!'

Hobo's face drained of its colour.

'Blimey. That's a bit steep actually. I don't think I should.'

'Yes, well, to be honest, it is a lot to ask for a coat,' said Lucy.

Mr Protheroe raised both his hands, as if to

confess something to the kids.

'You're right. Absolutely. I mean, you can get a decent coat around here for twenty-five, thirty quid. But can a thirty quid coat do this?'

He took Hobo's wrist and pressed a small round button on the cuff. Lucy and Hobo watched and waited. Suddenly, Hobo looked really surprised for a second, and then he burst into a massive grin.

'Wow!' gasped Hobo. 'It's getting warmer! It's like an electric blanket! This is amazing!'

'Good, isn't' it?' said Mr Protheroe. 'That's not all... Check this out!'

He pressed another button beside the first. The coat glowed slightly and its surface became clear, as if it was made of water. Lucy gasped as the surface reflected the rest of the room. It was like a magic trick – as if the coat was trying to camouflage itself to look like its surroundings. The same way she'd seen some fish and octopuses do in nature documentaries.

'I've got to admit – that IS amazing,' she said. 'How many batteries does it take?'

'No batteries, no electricity, nothing! It's self-powered, doesn't rip, and is one-hundred-percent waterproof. How's that grab you?'

'I'm grabbed,' said Hobo excitedly. 'I can see why everyone's buying them now!'

*

Five minutes later, and eighty-five pounds lighter, Hobo left Protheroe's Surf Shack in his new amazing technicolour dreamcoat. He beamed as they walked down the street. Next to him Lucy wrapped her equally colourful scarf around her neck several times.

'Right then, I suppose I'd better get back to the madhouse,' said Lucy. 'Mum's still cleaning up after Christmas. There's wrapping paper everywhere.'

'Fair enough,' said Hobo. 'We've had a brief moment of freedom and a catch up.'

Lucy stroked the arm of his new coat. It felt warm.

'Yep, and you've joined the fashion elite with your funky new clobber!'

Hobo feigned aloofness. 'Don't hate me 'cause you ain't me, *dahling!*' he declared, twirling pretentiously.

'Catch you tomorrow? That is, if I'm still worthy of being in your presence?' she mocked.

'Oh all right, as it's you…' said Hobo, trying not to laugh. 'See you tomorrow!'

They split up and headed to their respective destinations.

As Hobo walked on, he heard the sound of a car horn. Beside him, a large white van pulled up.

'All right, buddy?'

It was Mr Protheroe.

'Nice coat you got there!' he said with a laugh.

'Yeah, I love it. Cheers!' said Hobo. 'Are they still selling well?'

'Non-stop, mun! I'm off to Witches Point to pick up some more, in fact. Thought you might need a lift somewhere?'

'No thanks, I'm not far from home, but cheers anyway!' replied Hobo.

'Fair enough, butt. Just thought I'd ask,' said Mr Protheroe. He gave Hobo a wave and pulled away.

Lucy was also very close to home when she passed the newsagents. Dad had eaten all the Christmas biscuits. She slipped inside and grabbed some chocolate biscuits and milk. Mum would be pleased with her resourcefulness.

As she paid for the items, she looked down on the counter and saw a stack of newspapers. The headline said:

MISSING: COUNT RISES TO TEN!

Her first thought was of Hobo – with all these people going missing, it probably wasn't a good idea to split up and walk home alone. She sent him a text as soon as she left the shop.

Hobo didn't reply to it, which wasn't like him. So she called him. Hobo answered.

'Hi, Luce. What's up?'

'Hi. I just sent you a text. Did you get it?'

'Nope, nothing at all. That's weird. When – send it?' said Hobo. A word or two was missing from his sentence.

'Literally two minutes ago. Have you got a good signal there?' asked Lucy.

'Not – if – cause – maybe – home – later – 'kay?' came the fractured reply.

'You're breaking up. I didn't catch that,' said Lucy.

But all she heard was a high-pitched buzz and the call ended.

At the other end, Hobo looked at the screen of his phone in confusion: it was flickering strangely. He tried to call her back but all he could hear was a crackling sound. He shrugged and put it down to low battery or bad signal, and carried on walking.

When she got home, Lucy threw off her hat and scarf and went into the kitchen, where Mum was making dinner.

'Had a good time?' asked Mum, as Lucy put the new bottle of milk into the fridge.

'Yeah, wasn't bad,' said Lucy. 'We went to the café. And Hobo got a new coat.'

Mum turned around.

'Oh, talking of Hobo, did you see his mum on the

news?'

'Oh! We did see the news at the café, but didn't see Hobo's mum. There's ten people missing now. That's pretty scary.'

'It is, love. I don't like that the police haven't got to the bottom of it.'

'Yeah, I hope they turn up,' said Lucy. She decided to change the subject as she didn't like to see her mother worried.

'All right, Mum. I can see some dishes that need washing. Let me at 'em!'

She rolled up her sleeves and went to the sink.

As the sun went down over Witches Point, Mr Protheroe parked his van as close to the cliff as possible. It was cold and windy, and the sea spray hit him like rain, but he was undeterred from his mission. He was making far too much money to be put off by some bad weather.

He carefully made his way down the sloping cliff edge, and when he reached the bottom, he took a quick look around. It was quiet except for the wind and the waves. He pulled out a torch and headed for a cave in the side of the cliff. Illuminated by the beam were four more plastic crates of valuable sportswear. Mr Protheroe smiled. His ship had come in. Quite literally, in this case.

*

Hobo was nearing the end of town when he felt his phone buzzing in his pocket, and saw that it was Lucy.

'Hi, Lucy, can you hear me now?'

'Ah, that's better! Yes, I can. Listen, those missing people from town – there are ten missing now. We've got to do some research.'

'Absolutely, where do we start?'

'Well, let's make a list of the missing people. We'll compare notes and chat, okay?'

Hobo walked over to the doorway of an electrical store to get out of the wind while he talked.

'Maybe there's a link that connects all of them.'

'That's what I thought. I'll read the papers, make some notes and email them over to you.'

Hobo idly watched the TV screens in the window as he talked. They silently showed live programmes from a number of channels.

'Hobo?' said Lucy. 'Are you still there?'

'Oh, sorry, I was distracted. Yes, I'm here. Send me what you have and I'll take a look at it when I get in.'

'Aren't you home yet?' she asked, concerned. Hobo smiled.

'No, but it's fine. I'll get a move on, okay?'

'Don't talk to any strangers and don't stop.'

'Roger. Over and out,' said Hobo.

Hobo stepped out of the shop doorway and the

cold wind hit him once again. He shivered, but then remembered he could be warm in seconds with the push of a button. The coat warmed up just like before, and Hobo set off on the last leg of his walk home.

Unknown to him, the screens in the shop window began to shake and flicker – white noise obscuring the pictures.

After a few minutes of determined walking, Hobo could see his street in the distance. It was getting dark and he began to feel apprehensive, thinking about the ten people who had gone missing without a trace. Ogmore-by-Sea wasn't particularly known for a lot of crime, but in recent times he had witnessed some pretty strange things, and to be alone in the dark was a little spooky.

Unexpectedly, a bright yellow light grew in front of him. At first he thought it was an approaching car with yellow fog lights, but this light was too close and too silent to be a car. It appeared to be the same intense light that he and Lucy had seen when the little plastic soldiers had disappeared after the Christmas Fayre.

Probably not a coincidence, he thought.

Abruptly the light disappeared into a void, leaving a tall dark figure in front of Hobo. The figure seemed to have the face of a bearded dragon. It hissed, 'Do not move, criminal. You will pay for your transgressions.'

Lucy was busy on her laptop. She'd read the newspapers and written down as much important information about the missing people as she could. She'd even printed out a map of the town, and drawn circles to mark where the people lived, and also where they were last seen. But so far, there was no obvious pattern. This, she realised, was a perfect time to get Hobo's big brain onto the case. And refill her hot chocolate mug.

She went downstairs, where Mum was busy stuffing clothing into a black bin liner.

'Perfect timing!' said Mum. 'I'm taking these to the charity shop in the morning, but is there anything here you want to keep?'

'Oh, okay,' said Lucy, kneeling down on the carpet. She delved into the pile of clothes and began to examine them. She saw that most of them were clothes that she and Mum hadn't seen – let alone worn – since they moved to Ogmore-by-Sea.

It was sorted out in less than two minutes. Mum was surprised at how Lucy was less sentimentally attached to old clothes than she was. She held up a tatty brown duffel coat.

'Aww, are you sure about this? You had this when you were tiny!'

Lucy exaggerated a shudder. 'Ugh! I'm sure! How did I ever leave the house in that thing? It's hideous!'

Mum sighed. 'Oh well, I suppose it fulfilled its purpose. Lovely and warm though.'

Lucy jumped in sudden realisation – warm coat! Hobo!

'I've got to ring Hobo, Mum. Won't be long!'

When she got back to her room, Lucy grabbed her phone and noticed that she'd had two missed calls and four texts from Hobo – all in the last five minutes. She wondered if he'd found out something that she hadn't been able to. The texts became slightly more panicked as they went along:

Call me back ASAP!

Where are you? This is serious!

You won't believe what's happened – ring me!

This is really bad! Code Red! Where are you?

Lucy couldn't decide whether to feel excited or worried. She reasoned that if Hobo was making repeated attempts to contact her then he was at least all right and not missing with the others. She quickly called him and Hobo picked up within a fraction of a second.

'Hey, what's with all the—' she began, but she was cut off by Hobo's panicked stream of words.

'OhmygodLucyyouwon'tbelieveitIwasnearlyho meand—'

'HOBO! Slow down, okay?' said Lucy, trying to sound calming. 'Start again and remember to breathe!'

Hobo took a deep breath and started again, but he clearly sounded shaken.

'I was just about to go home, but there was this really bright flash of light. I thought I was about to get hit by a car, but it wasn't a car! It was a really tall… *thing*! It called me a criminal and tried to destroy me!'

'Go on!' she urged.

'It grabbed my arm, and I thought I was a goner, but I just slipped out of my coat to get away from him. I went through the back lanes and jumped into one of the green recycling bins behind the shops!'

'What was it like?' said Lucy, desperately.

'Dark and smelly! There was rotten food in there!'

'Not the bin, the thing that grabbed you!'

'Tall! Taller than my dad. It had scales and spikes all over it like a lizard! Definitely alien!'

'Where is it now?'

'I don't know. I couldn't see much from inside

the bin. It was just standing there, holding my coat, then the bright light flashed again and it was gone!'

'Thank goodness for that,' said Lucy.

'What's good about it? He stole my coat!'

'I meant at least you're all right. Stay by your computer. I'll send you my notes. And call me if anything else happens, okay?'

'Okay, will do. I need a bath first. I stink!'

'Oh yeah, fair enough! Catch you later!'

Lucy was massively relieved that Hobo was all right, but also a little scared at the thought of ten people being destroyed by alien invaders. She went back to her research with a new determination.

Mum popped in. 'Hi, what are you up to?' she asked.

'Not much, what's up?'

'Well, I wanted to talk to you about these missing people. I think maybe you should hang around the house for a couple of days – or at least stay very close.'

Lucy looked disappointed. 'But I've been in since Christmas Eve, if you don't count today.'

'I know,' said Mum, 'but until the police find out what happened, I think it's safer to stay nearby. Ten is a lot of people to just disappear. It's worrying.'

'Fair enough, I suppose. Oh, Mum?'

'Yes?'

'I wanted to ask you something. You know Hobo

bought a new coat today? Well, he lost it.'

'Oh dear, so soon? How did that happen?'

Lucy didn't like to lie, especially to Mum, but this was for a good cause. 'Well, we went back to the café, and he must've left it on the back of the chair. I think it got stolen. He really loved that coat. I was wondering if I could use my Christmas money to buy him a replacement?'

'But you said it was expensive?'

'Eighty-five pounds. I know it's a lot, but this would cheer him up. He's really down about it.'

'Well, I suppose so… If you're sure. I tell you what, I'll ask in the café if anyone's picked it up or handed it in. If not, I'll pop over to the shops and pick one up for you. I'm assuming he takes a large?'

'Yeah, that'd be brilliant. Thanks, Mum. He bought it in Protheroe's Surf Shack by the way.

'Did he now? Okay? Don't spend too long on the computer. Goodnight, Lucy.'

'I won't. Night, Mum!'

Mum went back downstairs, leaving Lucy to it.

Lucy woke up the next morning with a jolt, as if she'd been struck by lightning. Her first thought was to contact Hobo to check that the lizard men hadn't got him.

Thankfully, her phone already displayed a reassuring text.

All was well:

> Got your notes. Good stuff.

> No pattern yet.

> Still gutted that I lost my coat :(

That was a relief. Lucy went downstairs and saw Mum in the hallway putting her coat on. Beside her were two bin liners full of old clothes.

'Morning!' said Mum. 'Breakfast is on the table. Cornflakes or muesli. If you want toast, you'll have to wait until I get back, we're out of bread, I'm afraid.'

Lucy shrugged. 'Nah, it's fine, I'll have cornflakes. Are you going to the charity shop?'

'Yes, and the café, like I said. I won't be long. Will you promise me you'll stay in today? Someone else went missing last night.'

'Did they? Who was it?'

'Some teacher. Don't cheer! It's on the local news this morning.'

'I like all my teachers, Mum! Fine, I'll stay here. Is it okay if Hobo comes round?'

'Of course. See you in about half an hour. I've got my key.'

After Mum left, Lucy sat cross-legged in front of the

telly while munching on her cornflakes. The local news came on, leading with the story about the missing teacher.

'Today's top story. The disappearance of two more locals pushes the total of missing persons up to twelve,' said the newsreader.

Lucy was shocked. She'd counted ten, but with this teacher that should make eleven. But twelve now? She watched intently.

'Secondary school teacher Gareth Hutchinson was declared missing this morning after his wife reported his disappearance in the early hours. And a police officer, PC Melissa James has also joined the missing, as she failed to turn up at the station this morning. Police are doing all they can. A dedicated helpline has been set up…'

There was a loud knock at the door. Lucy jumped, nearly spilling her cornflakes over herself. She crept to the hallway and peeked cautiously around the doorway, just in case a seven-foot-tall lizard was there. Thankfully it was a familiar bald boy in a blue hoodie.

'There's a pattern, Lucy!' said Hobo excitedly, waving an exercise book full of post-it notes. 'I've found a definite pattern!'

Looking over his notes, Hobo explained his findings.

'Okay, well I compared the list of everyone

missing so far, except the teacher and the police officer, and I listed things they had in common. Firstly, they're all under thirty-five years old. They all live or work very close to the town centre, and they all went missing after dark or before sunrise.'

'So… what does that tell us?' asked Lucy.

'Well, for a start, we can eliminate a fair few of the population.'

'Okay, so what now?'

'Well, I'd say we talk to a few people who knew them and see what else we can find out.'

Lucy shook her head.

'Not going to happen, I'm afraid.'

'Why's that?'

'I'm confined to the house. Mum's worried and she's asked me to stay in today.'

Hobo took a second to think.

'Oh, I see. Well, I guess I can't do much about you being stuck indoors, but we have a big advantage over the police – we know aliens are involved! And aliens, my dear Watson, are our speciality!'

'You've got a point there. Okay, why don't we look up the two new missing people and see if they fit the pattern. We can do that here and maybe later you can speak to people in town.'

'Okay, good plan. So, Mr Hutchinson: Under thirty-five, lives and works in town, went missing during the night.'

'Check. And the police officer?'

'Well, I don't know how old she is, but yes, she lives and works in town, and she went missing before work this morning. That fits.'

Hobo suddenly had a brainwave and laughed.

'Why don't I just ask my mum?'

A quick text message exchange confirmed that PC James was indeed also under thirty-five. Just like the rest. But what did it mean?

'I need to hit the streets and ask some questions,' said Hobo.

'Tea and biccies first!' said Lucy. 'It's cold out there.'

Hobo nodded glumly.

'Yeah, well, I wouldn't be cold if I hadn't lost my coat to a lizard-thingy.'

Lucy went to the kitchen, calling back as she did so.

'One problem at a time, okay?'

Tea and biscuits was Lucy's diversionary tactic to keep Hobo there until Mum returned. Thankfully, she came back before Hobo had finished his cuppa.

'Hobo! Hello!' said Mum. 'How's life?'

'Hello, Mrs Wilson. I'm all right, thanks.'

'Lucy tells me you had a bit of bad luck yesterday.'

'Yeah. Spent all my Christmas money on this coat and then —'

Lucy coughed in an attempt to warn Hobo to avoid mentioning aliens.

'It got stolen. Or lost. Lost and stolen, really.'

'That's awful. Lucy told me about it. I asked in the café, but no one had seen it. Mind you, all the kids were wearing something similar. Bags and shoes too!'

Hobo sighed, a little more glumly. Lucy nodded at the shopping bag at her mum's side.

'Which is why…' said Mum, theatrically holding the bag out in front of her and delving into it like a magician searching a top hat, 'you might be interested in… this!'

She pulled out the coat proudly. Hobo jumped up in surprise.

'My coat! Oh my days! Where did you find it?'

'I didn't,' said Mum. 'It's a new one. Lucy saw how much you missed it and wanted to buy you a replacement. Which is a lovely thing to do.'

Hobo was even more surprised, and a little guilty.

'Lucy! You didn't have to!'

'Yeah, well, I wanted to. Merry Christmas!'

Hobo gave Lucy a big hug.

'Thank you so much! Both of you!'

'You're very welcome,' said Mum. 'But don't go losing this one, okay? I know they're all the rage at the moment, but goodness knows why they're so expensive!'

'Show her, Hobo!' said Lucy.

'All right,' said Hobo. 'Here, put it on and you'll see.'

Mum put the coat on, looking slightly confused. It fitted her well and was pretty comfortable.

'Well, it's nice enough, but I still can't say it's worth… Oh my goodness!' She felt the coat warm up as Hobo pressed the cuff button. 'Ooh, wow! That's handy!'

'And this,' said Hobo, pressing the second button. The coat's surface began to take on the colours and shapes of the surrounding room as if it was a mirror ball or a mosaic.

'Virtual camouflage? That's amazing! No wonder these things are so costly!' said Mum. She took the coat off and handed it back to Hobo.

'You'd better have it back. I could get used to that!' laughed Mum as she went to the kitchen.

Hobo noticed that Lucy was preoccupied, holding both her own and his phone in each hand. She looked at them then the television and back again a few times.

'What's up?' asked Hobo.

'Another discovery,' said Lucy. 'I've just found out why the phones have been playing up. It's the coat!'

'Are you sure? Show me.'

Lucy tossed Hobo his phone, which he dropped.

'Press one of the buttons and watch the screens.'

Hobo did so and all three screens flickered with interference. There was a faint high-pitched noise coming from the phone.

'Oh, wow. So the coat interferes with phones and TV. Interesting.'

'Can that help us?' asked Lucy.

'Maybe. We need to keep that in mind. It could be a clue.'

'All right. I guess you're off out to play investigative journalist now?'

Hobo put his coat on. 'Yes, I am. I'll see who I can find to talk to. I'll be back by… let's say three o'clock?'

'Gotcha. I'll see what I can do here, and we'll compare notes later. Good luck!'

'You too!'

'Don't get kidnapped by any lizards!'

'Not funny, Lucy!'

After Hobo left, Lucy made herself an extra large hot chocolate and hit the Internet with a vengeance. She searched for the names of all the missing people and pasted their addresses, information, ages, schools and anything else that she found interesting into a document for easy reading. She couldn't see much of a link between them, aside from the things they'd already established, but maybe their friends and family might reveal something to Hobo that made more sense.

An hour later, the only thing she'd managed to discover was that some of the missing people were into sports. Russ Price was a boxer. Hobo said that Alwyn Ashford was a runner. And Andy Shackleton and his girlfriend were members of the sports centre. While that might all be a coincidence, Lucy felt it could be handy to note down. Who knew what Hobo might have discovered?

She didn't have to wait long. Hobo called back a lot sooner than he'd said he would. Just before two o'clock, Hobo knocked the door, looking excited and a little bit nervous at the same time.

'Hey! You're back early,' said Lucy. 'What's up?'

'I think I've cracked it. Well, I'm almost entirely sure I've cracked it. Let me in, quick!' said Hobo, a little panicked.

'Sure. Let's go to my room. I don't want Mum to get freaked out if she hears anything… you know… out of this world, okay?'

'Sure, let's go,' said Hobo, already through the door. Lucy grabbed his arm.

'Wait! Where's your coat?'

'In a bin,' said Hobo. Lucy's jaw dropped.

'I'll explain upstairs.'

Hobo's tale grew a little darker with every sentence. Lucy listened with interest as he gave her a detailed account of the people he spoken to in town. Each one knew one of the missing, and they all had one thing in common.

'You're serious?' said Lucy, her jaw in danger of touching the floor.

'I'm serious,' said Hobo. 'It's the coats.'

Lucy put both her hands on her head to try and stop her brain from exploding. It was all falling into place. Hobo continued, but spoke a little quieter.

'Everyone I spoke to told me that the ten missing people had recently bought something from the Surf Shack. It's all the rage, isn't it?'

'Definitely. And that explains the sporty types who went missing,' said Lucy.

'And it's not just the coats,' added Hobo. 'The shoes and the bags, too. Some of the missing people had gloves and boots from the same place! They all had the warming-up buttons and the camouflage features!'

'And this signal attracts the aliens. They turn up and destroy people…'

'We don't know that,' interrupted Hobo. 'Maybe they just want their stuff back?'

'But the people are gone, Hobo!' said Lucy, forgetting to keep her voice down.

'Yeah, that's what worries me. And that's why my second coat is in a dumpster. Sorry, Luce.'

Lucy shook her head. 'No it's totally fine. I

would've done the same thing. But I just thought of something. Something really bad.'

'Already ahead of you,' said Hobo gravely. 'If pressing the button alerts the aliens… and they work at night… they'll come for more people tonight!'

'You're right, but we've already pressed a button. Here in this house! They might come for us as soon as it gets dark!'

'Oh no,' said Hobo. 'What are we going to do?'

What would Grandad do? He was never one to run or hide. He'd take action. Face the problem head on. That's what he'd do.

Lucy said nothing. She calmly stood up, pulled her woolly hat on and flung her ten-foot scarf around her neck.

'We're going to the Surf Shack. It's time we got abducted by aliens!'

Lucy and Hobo managed to get out of the house by persuading Mum to give them both a lift to Hobo's house. It was closer to Protheroe's Surf Shack and he didn't have to stay indoors.

At Protheroe's Surf Shack, Hobo peered through the window. There wasn't much left in the shop, and he couldn't see any sign of movement inside.

'What if Mr Protheroe is one of them?' said Lucy.

Hobo shook his head. 'He can't be. He's had this shop for years. Long before you moved here. Mum knows him. He's eccentric, but definitely human.

'Okay, that's something at least,' said Lucy with a sigh of relief. 'But if he's been selling all this stuff, and he's not here now... do you think they've got him?'

'Nope, not yet,' said Hobo confidently.

'How do you know?' asked Lucy.

Hobo pointed to a small piece of paper taped to the inside of the door's glass. It read,

GONE TO PICK UP STOCK.
BACK IN AN HOUR
NICK

'Argh! This isn't helping!' said Lucy in despair. 'We've got to just wait for him to get back? It'll be dark soon!'

Hobo rubbed his head. He often did this to kick-start his brain. This time, however, it didn't work. He frowned. 'I've got nothing. Sorry.'

Lucy huffed in defeat and sat down in the doorway. As she rested back on the door, it suddenly swung open, and Lucy rolled backwards into the shop.

Hobo followed her in, closing the door behind him. Lucy got to her feet and looked around.

'Maybe he is here after all?' said Lucy. 'Hello? Mr

P? Are you there?' she called, just to be sure. There was no answer.

'You know we're going to get done for breaking and entering if we get caught in here?' said Hobo worriedly.

'I know. He must've forgotten to lock up or something,' said Lucy. 'Better make this quick.'

'Make what quick?' asked Hobo.

Lucy found the plastic crates that contained some of the new clothes, bags, shoes and other items. She started pulling them all out and pressing the small wrist buttons on each one.

'Come on, give me a hand!' she called. Hobo did the same, but with a confused look on his face.

'Er... why are we...?'

'This should get us noticed, don't you think?' said Lucy, with a devious grin.

Within three minutes, the shop was illuminated in a bright yellow light. And a second later, the shop was empty. No Lucy, no Hobo, no new clothing.

The first thing Lucy and Hobo noticed was the smell. It was like new Wellington boots, or a raincoat. Yes, it definitely was a new plastic kind of smell.

Then they realised that they were aboard a spaceship. It was a wide and circular room, lit by a bright white circle above them. They couldn't see any doors or any kind of furniture. It was like being locked inside a cereal bowl, with another bowl on top.

Lucy wandered over to the wall. She put her palm on it and found that it was comfortably warm and vibrating gently.

Hobo took a few steps to look around, when suddenly three spotlights appeared on the floor in front of him. Then, from the lights, three very tall lizard-men rose up, passing through the floor like ghosts through a wall.

Lucy ran to Hobo's side. The middle alien spoke first in a thin, raspy tone.

'We are the Tribunal. You are criminals and will face judgement for your transgressions.'

Lucy gasped. It was always a bit mind-blowing to be in the presence of an actual alien. Hobo nearly gasped, but Hobo, however, spoke up, which was unusual as Lucy was usually the outspoken one.

'That's the second time you've called me a criminal! What have we done? We haven't broken any laws!'

He paused for a second, then added, 'Well, apart from trespassing in Protheroe's.'

The head lizard tilted his head sideways, like a dog would if one whistled at it.

'You do not fear us – and have much to say. Do you speak for your people?'

Hobo gulped. Standing up for himself was one thing, but it was a bit much to speak for all of humanity.

'Well, not really, but why are you destroying people for no reason?'

The lizards either side of the head honcho stepped forward, their scaly hands reaching out. But the leader put his arms out to stop them moving forward.

'Wait. This one intrigues me. Let us hear what it has to say.' The two others agreed and stood still. Their leader approached Hobo.

'We have every reason. This you know. But we will not destroy you. Too many have lost their lives. We will not stoop to your level of barbarity.'

Hobo looked at Lucy.

'Okay, I have no idea what's going on now.' Lucy stepped up, gripping the ends of her scarf in each hand tightly.

'We're not criminals. You've been taking people from their homes! Why?'

The leader seemed surprised to see Lucy speak. Hobo was different – still a primitive human, but he looked more evolved. Taller and less encumbered by fur, like the lizards. He thought Lucy was some kind of… pet.

'You speak, too? Fascinating. Very well, we shall read the charges as is your right.'

Lucy and Hobo watched as a holographic galaxy materialised in the air in front of them. It glowed blue and rotated slowly, showing tiny little flashes of light at random. Little planets and the occasional star exploded like tiny fireworks.

'The war against the Keskar is over. Your leaders have admitted defeat and surrendered. Your forces are scattered. You have lost. Now, it is our duty to locate and retrieve all remaining soldiers such as you, and prepare them for trial.'

He waved his hand and the galaxy faded away. Then all around the walls of the room, rectangular doors silently slid open, revealing small cubicles, in which stood all of the missing people from town. They looked asleep, still wearing their brightly coloured sportswear from Protheroe's Surf Shack.

'Lucy, look!' said Hobo in amazement. 'It's Alwyn Ashford and Russ Price! And the others. They're alive!' he gasped.

Lucy studied the faces of the people and looked back to the aliens. 'Are they?'

'Of course. As I said, no more will be slain. Your trial awaits in the Justice Arena at the Galactic Core.'

Lucy pointed at the sleeping townspeople in despair.

'But they're not criminals or soldiers! You've made a mistake! Can't you understand? These are ordinary people. They've never left Earth! We're not part of this war that you're on about!'

The leader seemed intrigued. He strode around the room, looking closely at his captives.

'Is this the truth? That you are not aiding the Keskar? Are you not an interstellar species?'

'That's right,' said Hobo. 'We've only been to the moon a handful of times and that was decades ago! 1972, if I remember correctly. Apollo Seventeen, I think!'

'Check your computers, your history books,' added Lucy. 'You must have a record of our history.'

The leader stopped looking at the sleeping figures and walked back to Lucy and Hobo.

'We do have access to the histories of many civilizations. But we are not concerned with the events on small, insignificant worlds such as yours. Why do you assume we would be taken in by your obvious attempts to lie?'

Hobo felt an unexpected rise of anger. 'Who are you calling insignificant?'

'Calm down, Hobo,' said Lucy. 'We're getting somewhere here!'

Hobo took a few deep breaths and went quiet.

'What he means,' began Lucy, 'is we're not completely unknown to other life forms. But we've never heard of these Keskar people.'

'Can you prove this, or are you just delaying the inevitable?' said the leader.

Lucy realised that she needed to prove that she was telling the truth, or she and Hobo would soon be snoring away in the cubicles, heading for a galactic trial light years away from Earth.

'Yes, I can prove it,' said Lucy with confidence. The kind of confidence that made Hobo feel a lot less confident at the same time. Whatever could she say or do to prove to this… thing that the Human Race wasn't involved in some space war?

'My grandad is known to many people and races outside the Earth. I'm sure that if you Google his name, you'll see that I'm telling the truth.'

'What is…"Google"?' asked the leader, tilting his head to one side again.

'I mean search, look up, cross-reference. Look for Lethbridge-Stewart. Brigadier, or just UNIT. See what your records say!'

The lizard henchmen waved their arms in the air. In front of them, two circular screens opened, floating in the air like the galaxy map. Hundreds of pages of information, written in strange symbols, flickered past.

Suddenly, the screens stopped moving. Lucy could see the familiar shape of an old logo – a circle with a smaller circle inside, shaded in with a grid of lines and the letters U – N – I – T curved around the top. She turned her head towards Hobo. 'Do you think the plastic soldiers were wanted criminals?'

she whispered.

'And were taken by these chaps. It would appear so,' Hobo whispered back. 'At least that's cleared that up.'

'Quiet!' The lizard's leader inhaled loudly.'You tell the truth, human. We know of your associate, and his dealings with galactic races. He is not allied to the Keskar.'

'He's not an associate, he's my grandad,' said Lucy.

'I can see he is a soldier, but he did not take part in this war. Where is this man? I wish to talk to him.'

Lucy's triumphant expression changed to gloomy in a second. 'He's… well, he's gone. He died. When I was a little younger.'

'This is unfortunate. You have my condolences. I see that he was, indeed, a respected leader among your people. It is becoming apparent that…'

The leader of the lizard men stopped mid-sentence. He looked up and down at Lucy, pausing in deep thought for a moment. Hobo looked at Lucy too.

'What's he doing?' asked Hobo. Lucy shrugged.

'No idea. I think he's humming.'

The lizard man was indeed humming. He had just discovered something very, very important and was wondering how best to proceed. Finally, he said a few words in an alien language to his two companions. They nodded and left the room, sinking into the floor like a biscuit into a cup of tea.

'You need not provide me with any more credentials. I am satisfied that you are truthful. But I still have questions to ask you.'

'Ask away,' said Lucy. 'My name is Lucy Wilson, by the way, and this is my friend—'

'Kostinen,' interrupted Hobo. 'Hobo Kostinen. Licenced to er... help.' He turned to Lucy. 'I've always wanted to introduce myself like that.'

The lizard held his palm up as if he was about to say 'hi'.

'I am Vorann of the First Tribunal. I offer you an apology for our mistake.'

'Apology accepted, Vorann,' said Lucy, holding her palm up too. Hobo did the same, except that he opened his fingers like Mr Spock.

'Live Long and Prosper,' said Hobo, with a perfectly straight face.

Vorann tilted his head in that same way again. Lucy cringed.

'Thank you, Kostinen. I certainly intend to,' said Vorann.

'So, Vorann – you said you had questions?'

'I do. Why do your fellow humans wear the uniform of the Keskar forces?'

Hobo put his hand up, as if he was in class.

'Ah, you're on about the coats and the trainers,

87

right? Well, everyone wears them because they've been sold in town at the Surf Shack.'

Lucy put the last piece of the puzzle together in her mind.

'Uniform? Ah! It's all army gear! Hobo, that's why they have heating and camouflage – this is intergalactic army surplus! It's true,' she said to Vorann. 'Everyone's been buying it. Not for war, just for fashion. They're very popular.'

'We are able to trace them upon activation. This is how we were able to capture the people you see around you. But where are the uniforms coming from?' asked Vorann.

'Beam us back down to our town, and I'll show you,' said Hobo.

With a flash of bewildering light, Lucy, Hobo and Vorann were standing back in Protheroe's Surf Shack. There was still no sign of anyone there. Vorann looked at the few items of Keskar military clothing strewn about.

'So this is the location of the shop keeper. Where is he?'

'Somewhere else, picking up stock, apparently,' said Lucy, 'but where that is, I don't know.'

'I remember him saying that he was off to Witches Point to pick up stock!' said Hobo. 'I don't think there are any warehouses or suppliers there though. It's just a bay and some cliffs.'

Lucy pointed at the plastic crates.

'Look – remember these? They're still covered in sand and bits of seaweed. They were wet when we first came in here. Why is that?'

Vorann leaned forward and cautiously sniffed the crate, which made Hobo smirk a little.

'Marine algae. Multi-cellular life and inorganic minerals. We can trace this sample back to the original location.'

'He's got a nose for detective work,' said Hobo.

'Oi!' whispered Lucy, though she did think it was pretty funny.

Vorann touched a thin silver bracelet on his wrist and the bright lights took them away again.

At Witches Point, Mr Protheroe was lifting the last crate of clothing into the back of his van when he saw the yellow beams all around him. He spun around and saw Lucy, Hobo and a seven-foot-tall lizard staring at him.

'Aagh! What's going on? Where did you come from?' he screamed in terror. Lucy tried to calm him down.

'Mr P! It's okay, it's okay! We need to talk to you about your stock! Relax!'

Mr Protheroe couldn't take his eyes off Vorann, which was understandable really.

'What's that thing? What is it?'

'This is er… well, he's kind of a police officer. Sort of,' said Hobo. 'Try not to panic, and everything will be cool, okay?'

Mr Protheroe realised that there was nowhere to run, and he wasn't even sure his legs would have worked anyway, he was so terrified. So he tried to slow his breathing down and waited for the creature to speak.

'You are in unlawful possession of Keskar military apparel and equipment. I am here to remove it.'

Hobo pointed to the cave where the crates were being stored.

'Look! They were all in there!'

'Seaweed and sand,' said Lucy.

Vorann stepped forward towards Mr Protheroe, who cowered in fear. 'Where did you obtain these items? Explain fully and you may be spared a severe sentence.'

Mr Protheroe raised a shaking arm and pointed out to sea. 'Out there! Back in the summer, I went diving off the boat. I went a bit too far out and I saw this shipwreck. Or maybe it was a submarine. I don't know! But there was this hole in the side. There were hundreds of boxes in there!'

'We can verify this,' said Vorann sternly. 'Be aware that mendacity will not be tolerated!'

Mr Protheroe nodded quickly. 'I'm not lying. I swear! I wasn't doing any harm! In fact, I was recycling, really! Cleaning up the sea! You know? Plastic pollution and all that!'

Hobo looked at Lucy. 'Good angle, I must say.'

Vorann turned to Lucy for confirmation.

'Does your planet have an issue with pollution within its hydrosphere?'

'Yeah,' said Lucy. 'It's pretty bad. But we are starting to do something about it though.'

Vorann tapped his bracelet and the sky darkened. The grey clouds above them all parted with a sound like thunder, and Vorann's huge spaceship came into view.

Even Lucy gasped as the giant metallic disc hung above the rippling sea, as if waiting for orders.

'Locate and retrieve the Keskar supply vessel and all remaining materials,' said Vorann, 'then bring me on board.'

The ship in the sky rotated like a turntable. Very slowly, it made half a turn, then it stopped. A triangular hole appeared in the underside, and the sea beneath it began to thrash about and boil. From under the water, another spaceship came into view. It was smaller and a dark red colour, encrusted with shells, seaweed, and mud. Lucy held onto her hat and Hobo watched in awe as the ship floated up into the bigger craft. Water and hundreds of fish gushed out of a crack in the side of the vessel.

Mr Protheroe pointed as it floated upwards.

'See? That's the ship! There's the hole where I found the boxes!' he shouted over the thundering noise and high winds.

The giant ship closed the triangular hole and rose up into the clouds again, disappearing from view. The winds died down and all was calm again. Except for Mr Protheroe, who was still traumatised from the experience. Lucy went to his side.

'Don't worry, it's over now. These people aren't invading or anything, they're just trying to clean up after a war. What you were selling was basically stolen goods – alien army surplus.'

'But that stuff made me a fortune! What am I going to do now?' asked Mr Protheroe sadly.

Vorann spoke up. 'You are going to consider yourself fortunate that you enjoyed some financial returns from these items and that we have not decided to charge you with unlawful possession of them.'

'Aye, fair enough, mate. I'll be off then,' said Mr Protheroe, closing the back door of his van. Vorann put a hand on his shoulder. He indicated Lucy and Hobo.

'Were it not for these ambassadors and their explanations of what has happened here, you would not be a free man. Remain here for a moment.'

'All right. Whatever you say,' said Mr Protheroe quietly.

Vorann turned to Lucy and Hobo.

'On behalf of the Tribunal, I thank you for your assistance. We are satisfied that this world is not involved in the war or its aftermath. We will return your people to you and remotely deactivate the tracing signals from the sold items. However, we cannot allow knowledge of our involvement here to remain in the memories of the people involved.'

'So you're going to mind-wipe the missing people in your ship and let them go?' asked Lucy.

'Yes. This is a simple and harmless procedure. Mr Protheroe will also have no memory of these events.'

'But what about us?' asked Hobo, worriedly. 'Are you going to do the same to us as well?'

'No, Kostinen. We would not perform a procedure on someone so important. Your memories will remain unaltered.'

Hobo smiled broadly. This would be one amazing memory to keep.

Vorann got down on one knee in front of Lucy. For a surreal moment, Lucy thought he was going to ask her to marry him, but that wasn't his intention.

'You are the latest in a line of noble human beings that represent your race in the wider universe. Your honesty and willingness to help makes you a credit to your species, and to the memory of your grandfather. You act responsibly and appropriately, for one who wears the sash of the Great One. Thank you, Lucy Wilson, and farewell.'

Lucy just smiled and watched as Vorann stood up, took a few steps back and touched his bracelet again. In a flash of yellow light, he was gone.

'Blimey. What a speech,' said Lucy.

'I think you impressed him,' said Hobo.

Mr Protheroe shook his head and looked over at the two kids.

'Hiya, kids! I'm about to drive back into town. Too cold to stay out here, isn't it? Want a lift?'

'Oh, okay then, thanks, Mr P,' said Hobo.

'You're Megan's boy, aren't you? I know your mother! She was a big help when I had a break-in at the shop. Call me Nick,' said Mr Protheroe. It was obvious that he had no memory of what had just happened. Vorann's mind-wipe had been instantaneous.

They got into Nick's van and headed back. Suddenly, Lucy spotted something very surprising.

'Stop the van!' she yelled.

Nick stopped the van and everyone got out.

In the early evening mist, ten people stood beside the road, looking lost and confused. The missing people had been returned to Earth as promised.

'Need a lift, you lot?' called Nick. 'I'm going back

into town.'

'That's very kind of you, mate,' said Russ Price, the boxer. 'Don't ask me how I got out here, I think I probably had one too many last night!'

'Jump in the back, plenty of room!' said Nick, opening the back of his van, which was now empty.

As everyone piled in the back, Hobo turned to Lucy.

'One thing... What did Vorann mean by "the Sash of the Great One"?'

'No idea,' said Lucy blankly. 'Maybe he meant this ridiculous scarf?' she laughed.

'Well, I'm going to need your help, O Great One,' said Hobo as it started to snow. 'I've got to get my coat from out of a dumpster...'

IMPOSTERS

Keren Williams

L ucy's head jolted, her eyes suddenly alert. Blinking furiously, she straightened herself and glanced hastily over at her friend in the passenger seat. Hobo swiftly turned his head towards the frosty sloped street on his left, trying his best to stifle a laugh and hide his smile.

I don't think Hobo saw, Lucy thought. *I hope I wasn't snoring.*

'And... we... are... here.' Mrs Kostinen pulled up next to the terraced house with red bricks, and cranked the handbrake into place.

The three of them unbuckled and slid carefully out onto the slushy pavement. Hobo's little brother, Gav, sat with his eyes glued to his Nintendo until Mrs Kostinen opened the door and tried to help him out of the car.

Finally out in the frostbitten air, Gav suddenly realised where they were, ran straight through the gate of the nearest house and up to the front door. Stretching up on his toes, he rang the bell. Lucy just hoped he had the right house; they all looked the same to her.

A short older lady, only a head or so taller than Lucy, answered the door. She seemed concerned, but as soon as she saw Gav grinning up at her the most welcoming smile filled her face and crinkled the unease from her eyes.

'Well, it can't be? It can't be my little Gavin?' The

old lady stooped slightly as Gav fell forward into her arms.

'Granny!' he squealed.

'Why, haven't you grown? You're almost up to my chin!'

Gav grinned up at her once more, before running through the door into the warmth of the house. It was Hobo's turn next.

'Hello, *cariad*,' she cooed, squeezing him tight before looking to Lucy with kind eyes. 'And you must be Lucy?'

Lucy nodded, and even though they had never met before, she was hugged just like the rest.

A pot of tea was made and twenty large cookies were placed on a plate in the centre of the small kitchen dining table. Hobo helped himself to six. Lucy ate three, nibbling at them daintily in an attempt at being polite. Gav and Mrs Kostinen only managed two, and Hobo's gran cut one in half on a flowery pink China plate and put the rest aside for later.

'I'm stuffed.' Hobo patted his belly. 'For now.'

Lucy rolled her eyes at her friend, secretly marvelling at how much food he could put away in one day. He'd been munching on sweets the whole ride over too!

'Come on, Luce, I'll show you around.'

Lucy and Hobo grabbed their rucksacks from the

hallway floor, kicked off their shoes and made their way up the cream carpeted stairs. At the top, the landing was of a medium length with four white-painted wooden doors placed evenly along it.

'This is the bathroom,' Hobo began, pushing open the nearest door. 'This one is Gran's,' he continued, pointing to the different rooms. 'Then it's mine and Gav's next to that.' Hobo rolled his eyes and sighed before stopping at the last door. He was not looking forward to sharing a room. 'And this one's yours.'

'Right, you two,' Mrs Kostinen called up the stairs. 'I'm off. Be good for Gran!'

Lucy and Hobo dumped their stuff and ran downstairs to say goodbye.

'See you next year,' Hobo joked, as his mum left the house. 'Come on, Luce, we've not finished yet.'

After a brief glance at the very festive living room, the pair returned to the kitchen-diner.

'Gran, can I show Lucy the basement?'

'Yes, but watch out for the monster down there.' Hobo's gran frowned down at the cookies on the table; only three were left. 'I think he may have gobbled the rest of these.' She chuckled as she began placing the remaining cookies into a tin.

Lucy followed Hobo down the stairs to the basement. The stairs creaked as they went.

If there is a monster down here, Lucy thought as they

reached the last step, *it definitely knows we're here now!*

The basement wasn't as spooky as Lucy expected it to be; in fact, it was actually quite cosy. The room opened out to the left of them, with a three piece suite positioned in the centre, complete with a coffee table, a big shaggy rug, and a TV that hung from the opposite wall.

Similar to the living room upstairs, the room had been adorned with Christmas decorations. There was a medium-sized Christmas tree with the largest golden star on top, and red reindeer-patterned cushions on the sofa.

The room almost reminded Lucy of Santa's workshop; to the right, two solid wooden workbenches lined the wall. The benches were scattered with paint pots, brushes, tools and wooden knick-knacks.

Lucy walked over to the benches for further inspection.

'Don't touch, it's not dry yet,' came a deep, accented voice from behind them.

Lucy hadn't noticed another person in the room. The man was tall, possibly in his sixties, with lots of grey threading through his once jet black hair. He wiped damp hands on his trousers as he walked towards them. It was at this moment that Lucy noticed three doors over to the far left of the room.

One led to the laundry room, the second was closed, and the third led to another bathroom.

'Grandad,' Hobo announced. 'This is my friend, Lucy.' Hobo's grandad greeted her with a small but sad smile.

'What have you been working on?' Hobo asked, filling the silence.

'Oh, nothing much. Just a bit of painting, but I've managed to misplace my favourite brush. It really has been the year for it.' Hobo's grandad scratched his head before rummaging through the objects scattered along his workbench.

'The year for it?' Lucy questioned.

'It's not just been a missing sock or two – that I can deal with – darn things always have a tendency to run off. But, no, I've lost paint brushes, tools, my reading glasses, and probably worst of all this year, my front door key. We had to have the locks replaced. Next thing, I'll be losing my mind!' He sighed and gave up his search. 'I'll just go see if your gran wants me to pop down the chippie for our dinner,' he muttered before climbing the stairs.

Lucy and Hobo looked to each other quizzically.

'I wonder—' Hobo began, but that was all he had time for.

'Hobo, Hobo!' Gav interrupted, bounding down the steps. 'Santa stopped here too. Quick!' he pleaded, before he ran back up the creaky steps.

*

After a hearty meal of sausage, egg and chip shop chips, the evening turned to board games, hot chocolate and a few too many sweets.

'That's a five letter word on a triple word score and one three letter word with a double letter score on "z". And I've used up all of my letters, so that's an extra fifty points, too.'

'Is it my turn yet, Hobo?' Lucy asked impatiently, as he counted up his score.

'Patience is not an absence of action; rather it is "timing". It waits on the right time to act, for the right principles and in the right way. Patience is power.'

Lucy rolled her eyes and placed three tiles on the board.

'Hmm… I'm not sure if that's a word. Let me just check the dictionary,' Hobo said, eyes wide with excitement.

Lucy groaned. Why did his grandparents have to buy him a Scrabble dictionary for Christmas? He was too smart for his own good without it, let alone with it.

'No, "Ympe" isn't a Scrabble-approved word. I wonder if it *is* a word though…'

'I don't think I can go,' Lucy decided sleepily, pulling her hands into the sleeves of her new Christmas jumper.

'I think it's time for bed anyway,' Hobo's gran

chimed in as Lucy tried to suppress a yawn. No one argued.

Snuggled in her pyjamas, Lucy sighed loudly into the darkness. She'd forgotten to go to the toilet and, suddenly having remembered, it was now all she could think about. She fought the urge to go for as long as she could, but it was no use. She was going to have to remove herself from the warm little nest she'd made.

Lucy walked along the corridor to the bathroom, but light shone from the crack under the closed door. Lucy bounced from one foot to the other. One minute passed, then two, then three, before she sighed and tiptoed her way down the stairs. It felt like she was being followed, but she knew it was just like the darkness playing tricks on her. She had no idea where any of the light switches were, so she felt her way down each step and along the walls until she was in the basement.

Lucy walked tentatively across the room and found herself in front of the three doors. She racked her brain. *Which one was the bathroom?*

Creak!

Lucy turned around slowly, but she couldn't see anything through the darkness.

All the bells on the Christmas tree rang out at once, making Lucy jump.

Pulling open the door closest to her, she fumbled for the light. Hobo's gran had warned them of a monster. And something was definitely in the darkness.

Lucy found the switch, but there was no bathroom.

The skull of a horse, with its mouth wide open, red ears and large bulging eyes, shot out towards her. A small giggle echoed in the darkness behind her.

Lucy screamed and scrambled backwards. Straight into something else, something that grabbed her!

'Lucy, Lucy, calm down. It's me, it's Hobo!' Hobo flicked the switch on the wall next to the cupboard, illuminating the basement.

'That's no monster, Lucy,' Hobo started to explain. 'That's the Mari Lwyd.'

'What's all this noise?' Hobo's gran said, the basement steps creaking rapidly as she strode quickly down them, with Hobo's grandad at her heels.

'It's th— the Marry Lloyd?' Lucy stammered, her heart still racing.

'The *Mari* Lwyd,' Hobo repeated, before he burst out laughing.

'Ahh, you've found my little friend, have you?' Hobo's grandad said.

Lucy nodded her head as he pulled out what

looked like a terrifying version of the hobby horse. The horse was wrapped in a white sheet, its pole hidden beneath, and was decorated with colourful reins, bells and ribbons.

'Yes, the Mari Lwyd, or *Y Fari Lwyd* as us Welsh like to call her,' Hobo's grandad explained. 'Old Mari here is said to bring good luck, though we've not had much of that have we, Vic?'

Hobo's gran shook her head. 'No, and I doubt she's going to start bringing luck just because she's out. Let's put her back where she came from. I don't know why old Stan left the Mari to you. All she's useful for is cluttering up my cupboard,' she declared with a slight shudder.

Hobo's grandad leaned the Mari up against the wall in the cupboard and sighed. 'I really don't know either.'

They all climbed back up the creaky stairs to their beds.

Lucy hid beneath her duvet, her heart slowing but her face still warm. *I'm a Lethbridge-Stewart, I shouldn't be scared over silly things like that*, she thought, kicking herself at how ridiculous she'd been. *And I didn't even go to the bathroom!*

But she wasn't getting out of bed again. Lucy let the warmth envelop her and she drifted drowsily off to sleep.

*

Lucy sat at the table for breakfast the next day still feeling a little embarrassed. Hobo sat beside her with two slices of toast and a bowl of cereal. She hoped he wouldn't bring up what had happened.

'What was all that about last night?' Hobo asked.

Lucy had hoped too soon. 'I just needed to use the bathroom, but someone was in there, so I thought I'd use the one downstairs.'

'But no one was in the bathroom upstairs.'

'Someone was, the light was on,' Lucy replied.

'No, I was last in and I turned it off before I went to bed—'

'It's the last day of the year. What are you two going to do?' Hobo's gran asked, noticing Lucy's discomfort.

'I was thinking of showing Lucy the park,' Hobo said through a mouthful of food.

'Well, be sure to wrap up warm. It snowed last night,' Hobo's gran warned, just as a mug fell from the kitchen counter.

She jumped. 'How on earth did that happen?'

Lucy heard a noise, almost like a giggle, and saw something race into the hall from the corner of her eye. Hobo jumped up to collect the fragments of the mug as his gran hurried out to fetch the mop. Lucy rushed after her, but as she rounded the corner into the hall, she was met with two shiny yellow eyes.

'Oh, it's just a cat,' Lucy muttered. She decided she needed to calm down. She threaded her fingers through her thick hair, pushing it away from her face. 'Do you need a hand?' Lucy called down the hall. All of her recent adventures had started to make her jumpy. She just needed to calm down.

Once everything had been cleared, Hobo tore through the last of his food and quickly pulled his thick hat onto his hairless head. It was time for a very cold winter's walk.

Hobo and Lucy pulled on layer after layer by the front door. Their new woolly Christmas jumpers were hidden by their large coats and scarves.

'You're not wearing your impractically long scarf,' said Hobo. 'Any reason?'

'Because it was impractically long. I can't imagine what kind of person would wear it.'

'Probably someone who wants to be noticed when they walk into the room.'

With hats pulled down tight on heads and fingers wrapped up warm, Hobo opened the door to the snowy Welsh village.

'Don't worry, Luce. There's no Mari Lwyd behind this door!' Hobo chuckled.

'Hold on, you've got a bit of...' Hobo's gran pulled a handkerchief from inside her cardigan sleeve, dabbed it quickly on the end of her tongue and began rubbing at Hobo's cheek.

'Gran!' Hobo cringed as he struggled sideways through the door, wiping furiously at his face. Frowning, he backed away from the house, turning a brilliant crimson as he went.

Hobo's gran winked at Lucy as she followed her embarrassed friend outside.

'You two have fun,' she called with a little wave, before shutting the door.

Lucy tried her hardest, but couldn't contain her laughter anymore. Hobo was still as red as a Mirror Clown's nose.

Her laughter didn't ease until they were four houses down and Lucy spotted a middle-aged woman standing at her door, repositioning the wreath that hung from it. Lucy smiled as they passed, remembering her dad trying to hang the wreath on their door – he'd managed to turn it into an oval and had pulled all the decorations off; it had looked a very sorry sight when he'd finished. In answer to Lucy's smile, the woman frowned at them and scurried inside, before slamming the door behind her – knocking the wreath to the cold concrete floor.

'What was that about?' Lucy asked.

They carefully continued down the slightly sloped street, trying to avoid the patches of ice. The world seemed still and silent, surprising for New

Year's Eve, but it wasn't long before the silence was broken.

'Where have you put him?' an older woman, wrapped up in a thick coat, challenged.

'Excuse me?' The middle-aged man, at whom the question was directed, looked perplexed.

'You've stolen him, haven't you? Where have you put him?'

'What on earth are you talking about?'

'Don't act like you don't know. You've been stealing from me for ages now!'

'You mean one of your hideous garden gnomes?'

'Of course I mean my garden gnomes. And they are *not* hideous!'

Lucy and Hobo stood still and silent, watching as the pair bickered over their neighbouring wall.

'Oh, you're one to talk! I'm missing half of my garden tools.'

'I've not taken anything from you,' the woman declared.

'Well, they sure didn't just walk off, did they?' the man announced, pointing an accusatory finger towards the woman. 'But that's probably what's happened with your silly little gnomes. They got fed up with you and walked away!' On that note the man, red with rage, opened the garden gate leading to the street and stormed away – his hot breath leaving billowing clouds in his wake.

The older woman rubbed her gloved hands together, before picking up one of the remaining garden gnomes and carrying it inside.

The street was silent once more.

Lucy and Hobo continued down the street and crossed the road to a large, very open playing field. Fenced off in the centre was a little park.

'I always come here when I visit. It's the best thing to do around here,' Hobo explained as he opened the gate to the park.

Lucy walked over to the swings first. She was about to sit down but the swing was frozen stiff. As for the other swing, it had been wound right up to the top.

Shrugging, she managed to crack a patch of ice from the first swing, creep up behind Hobo without him realising, and drop the ice down his back. He squealed and jumped. Lucy had not only managed to get it down his coat, but down his hoodie and t-shirt as well!

Hobo shook out his clothes, trying to coax the half-melted ice down his cold back. A little laugh came from somewhere behind Lucy. She turned to see who was there.

The park was deserted.

Hobo turned to Lucy. 'Right, it's on!'

Lucy's eyes opened wide as Hobo bent down and scooped up a ball of snowy-slush. It was fight or flight. Lucy ran past the muddy roundabout to the safety of the mud covered slide and started scooping up snow.

Snowballs pelted the slide with a twang.

Better the slide than me, Lucy thought. *With any luck maybe the snow will wash away the mud.*

Hobo could see Lucy's hair sticking out from behind the slide, but he couldn't quite get her.

There wasn't much snow under the slide and, having only been able to pack two tiny clumps of snow together, Lucy decided she had to make a run for it! Only daring to stick her head out a fraction, she tried to remember the layout of the park. There really wasn't anywhere to hide; she would have to go through the gate and take the war into no man's land.

Lucy sucked in a breath of cold air.

One.

She pulled her hat down as far as it would go.

Two.

She picked up her puny snowballs.

Three.

She made a run for it.

Dodging the snow and hurdling the broken spring riders, she had a clear line to the gate. Luckily for Hobo, the gate opened inwards, so there would be a brief pause as Lucy opened it. This would be his best chance.

Lucy hadn't been hit yet, and she was coming up

to the gate.

Was it a push or a pull? she thought as her hands collided with the gate, hoping it was the former. It wasn't! Lucy moved out of the way of the gate and pulled, just as Hobo threw a curveball that hit her right behind the knee, making her leg jolt.

'Hey!' Lucy shouted as she turned to look at her attacker, but Hobo wasn't taking any notice as he quickly packed more snow together.

Lucy had no choice. She would have to keep running. *Find a safe place, pack snow, get him back,* Lucy thought.

Lucy flew through the gate and across the field. Hobo wasn't far behind, snowballs flew in all different directions. One rushed straight past Lucy's ear, narrowly missing a rabbit.

'Hobo, stop!' Lucy shouted, looking concerned. As she turned the very last snowball collided with her shoulder, splattering her face with snow.

'A victory shot!' Hobo laughed. 'I suppose I've got you back now, Luce, and there was no way you were going to beat me anyway.'

'I definitely would have, I hadn't even started! I only shouted stop because you almost hit a rabbit.' Lucy turned around and pointed to the furthest end of the field, where it turned into a small woodland area. There, in front of the trees, were loads of little rabbits!

'Are you sure they're rabbits?' Hobo questioned.

'Well, what else would they be?'

'I don't know, but they look a bit… odd.' Hobo took a few steps forward to try and get a closer look. 'Their ears are really pointy and they don't look like they have any fur.'

Lucy could see that he was right. They both moved closer, as slowly and quietly as they could manage. The snow crunched under their shoes and it wasn't long before they had been spotted. Lucy and Hobo froze. Big, white eyes fixed on the two friends. It was a standoff!

After a few minutes, Lucy decided it was about time someone made a move and picked her right foot off the ground. But it hadn't even returned to the surface before the little creatures picked themselves up on their hind legs, made a horrible giggling noise and ran off into the trees, like tiny hunched-over humans.

Lucy and Hobo ran as fast as they could, but the little creatures were faster. It was obvious that they weren't rabbits, as they sprang over fallen trees and large roots with their strange feet. Too soon the creatures were out of sight, each one having bounded away in a different direction.

Lucy and Hobo stopped. Trying to catch them was pointless.

'What were they!?' Lucy panted, repositioning

the woolly bobble hat on her head.

'I don't know, but they could run! Did you see their legs?'

Lucy grimaced at the thought. They had been long, bald and gangly.

'Hey, what's this?' Lucy bent over and unearthed something red and green from beneath the snow. 'It's a gnome!' Lucy exclaimed as she brushed the dirt from its once rosy cheeks.

'I think there's something over here too.' Hobo took four paces towards something that looked like two black twigs poking out of the snow. He bent down and pulled gently at one of the twigs until both came free from Mother Nature's clutches. 'I think these are my grandad's reading glasses. I remember the frames.'

Lucy stood up and walked past Hobo towards the roots of a large fallen tree, surrounded by large planks of wood. It looked like a child's abandoned den.

Lucy pulled hard at one of the planks of wood. It had become stubborn with time, but with a crack of a few ivy stems and tree roots, the plank finally budged.

'Hobo, look at this!' Lucy beckoned.

Hobo wiped the lenses of his grandad's glasses before pocketing them and joining Lucy. Inside, the den was filled with a collection of objects, including paintbrushes, tools, garden gnomes, socks, money, keys, mobile phones, ribbons, dog leads, children's toys, wing mirrors and even a shoe!

'It's those creepy rabbits. They've been stealing from everyone!' Lucy shook her head at the piles and piles of stuff laced between the roots of the large oak tree.

Out of breath from rushing home, Hobo rang the bell to his grandparents' house. Hobo's gran opened the door, but her words were drowned out by the sound of Gav crying.

'What's going on?' Hobo asked.

'Oh, he's lost his Nintendo. We've turned the living room upside down looking, but we can't find it anywhere. He only had it about ten minutes ago...'

Hobo's grandad came down the stairs. 'It's not in the bedroom,' he announced. 'I think I saw him playing with it down in the basement earlier. I'll go and look down there.'

'We can help,' Lucy offered, as Hobo's gran tried to soothe the screaming Gav by offering him the last of the homemade cookies. This placated him for a moment, until Hobo's gran took the lid off the cookie tin and he reached in to find it empty. Gav started crying louder than before.

'I'll grab the sweet tin,' Hobo's grandad suggested, walking off into the kitchen.

Lucy and Hobo took off their damp clothes and shoes as quickly as possible and rushed down to the basement to get away from the sobbing. It didn't seem to help much.

They started rummaging around the room, crossing their fingers that the Nintendo would turn up soon.

'So what were those things in the woods?' Lucy said. 'And why have they been stealing from everyone in the village?'

'I don't think that's all they've been doing,' Hobo muttered.

'What do you mean?'

'Well,' Hobo continued, 'don't you think it's a bit strange that we weren't able to use anything in the park?'

'The frozen swing!' Lucy picked up one of the sofa pillows and threw it back down. 'And the mud on the roundabout and slide!'

Hobo nodded. 'Exactly!'

'Those pesky things!' Lucy announced. 'Stealing and ruining everyone's fun.'

'Yep.' Hobo sat down in a slump on the sofa. 'That's why I give up. I bet you the Nintendo is with all the other treasures in that den by no—'

'He's got a pair of lungs on him, I'll give him that.' Hobo's grandad laughed.

'Now, what's all this talk about treasure and

strange creatures?'

Lucy and Hobo froze. How were they going to get out of this one? The only adult that Lucy thought would truly understand was her own grandad. He'd fought many a monster in his time, but since he was no longer around that wasn't something worth thinking about. They had never, *ever*, dreamed of telling another adult, and especially not a family member, about any of their adventures.

Hobo's grandad sat in the armchair beside the sofa, watching them so closely it felt like their skin was burning. They had to say something, but what?

'Oh, it's nothing, really. We were just messing about.' Hobo smiled up at his grandad, willing him to accept his answer.

He laughed loud. 'I've always been able to tell when you're lying to me, Hobo. Right from when you were little.' Lucy looked to her friend; she thought she knew too. She'd only seen it happen a few times, mainly in times of trouble, but Hobo would very occasionally flick the nail of his thumb and second finger together, making them click once or twice before speaking.

Hobo looked quizzically over at Lucy.

What should we do? Lucy thought, looking back at Hobo's grandad. He seemed closed off, but his face was friendly. She imagined, even with the lack of hair, that Hobo would grow up to be an exact replica of him.

Lucy caught Hobo's grandad's eyes briefly. They sparkled, just like her grandad's used to. And she did something that she never thought she would do. She told him everything...

Hobo's grandad stared at the two of them.

'So you're telling me there are these creatures that have been stealing everyone's things?'

'Yep, all sorts of things,' said Lucy. We found garden gnomes, dog toys, sweets, books...'

'And these.' Hobo produced the glasses from inside his hoodie pocket.

Hobo's grandad took them, his face frozen, and rubbed the still-grimy lenses.

'But we have no idea why they're stealing them or how to stop them.' Lucy sighed and flopped backwards into the comfort of the sofa cushions.

They sat in silence. Were they in trouble? Was Hobo's grandad going to laugh at them and tell them to stop being so ridiculous?

He rubbed his chin, suddenly deep in thought. 'It's her, it has to be, its old Mari,' he whispered under his breath.

'What do you mean, Grandad?' Hobo asked.

'Ever since my old friend Stan passed away there's been weird goings-on all over the village. It started off small, almost unnoticeable, and now neighbours are falling out. People have been moving because of it. Heck, your own gran has been scared of opening our own front door!' Hobo's grandad rested his arms on the armrests and sat back. 'I always thought the tradition of the Mari was just a bit of fun for New Year's...'

'Can I borrow your laptop please, Grandad?'

Lucy could see her friend's brain working a mile a minute.

Hobo dragged the chunky laptop out from under the coffee table and within minutes he'd fired the old thing up and was typing frantically.

'Look here...' Lucy leaned in towards Hobo to get a better look at the screen. He'd opened up a few articles.

The darkest time of the year is traditionally when the veil between this world and the 'otherworld' is thinner, and so beings from that world can readily pass through to this one. In Celtic mythology, animals that had the ability to cross between this world and the underworld are traditionally white or grey-coloured.

Traditionally a New Year's Eve celebration, the Mari Lwyd and her group go from house to house trying to gain access through the performance of a series of verses. The inhabitants of the houses, after trying to outwit the Mari with their own verses, eventually grant her access, conferring luck on the household for the coming year and scaring away anything unwanted from the previous year.

Underneath the article was a picture from the 1900s. It showed a group of villagers in their Sunday bests. The person in the centre appeared to be the leader. He was holding the Mari, and next to him were two Punch and Judy type characters.

'So what's come through from the otherworld? Were those things we saw demons?' Lucy asked.

'Possibly some variation of one,' Hobo answered.

'But they were so small.'

'True, so what mythical creatures do we know of that are small?'

'The only ones I can think of are fairies and goblins.'

Hobo typed 'mythological being similar to a fairy or demon' into the search engine. He scrolled down the list of creatures.

'Stop, that's it. I think that might be them,' Lucy declared. 'It says here, "fond of pranks and misleading people".'

Hobo continued, '"The attendants of the devil are sometimes described as 'imps' and are often mischievous." Imps, yes that must be them!' Hobo scrolled down through the article.

During the time of the witch hunts, supernatural

creatures such as imps were sought out as proof of witchcraft, though often the so called imp was merely a black cat, lizard, toad or some other form of uncommon pet.

'I bet that's why they looked so much like rabbits to us at first,' Lucy said. 'They've learned how to hide themselves. And I bet it was an imp that pushed your gran's mug off the counter this morning. I thought I saw something, but when I looked all I could see was the cat!'

Hobo nodded in agreement and clicked through a few images to compare with the rabbit-like creatures. Although they weren't exactly the same, Hobo was pretty certain that they were the creatures they'd seen.

There was a large crash!

Lucy and Hobo turned, startled. Hobo's grandad stood, the Mari clutched in his hand. They'd not even seen him move.

'I have to carry on the tradition. Those pesky imps got in last year. Who knows what could get in this time.' His eyes sparkled brighter than before.

'But, how do we know whether the Mari will be enough?'

'We don't, but we have to try. It's New Year's Eve, so it's now or it's never.'

Later that day, Lucy and Hobo both pushed a wheelbarrow each up the sloped street, leaning as far forward as possible, to use as much strength as they could muster. It was their last trip to the community hall. They had managed to collect every single strange item they could find from the den, with no sign of any imps.

'Do you think the plan will work?' Lucy queried.

'Well, from everything we've researched, I don't see why not,' Hobo said, panting slightly. 'The Mari is supposed to scare away anything unwanted from the last year.'

'And those imps are definitely *not* wanted,' Lucy finished. She had been longing for an adventure before the Christmas holidays, but she hadn't anticipated four adventures in a row. *Be careful what you wish for!* she thought.

They finally reached the door to the community hall and, after catching their breath, they both pushed their wheelbarrows into the large, almost-empty room. Over to the left were three large tables covered in the miscellaneous items that Lucy and Hobo had brought in earlier . All they had to do was find room for the rest of the stuff on the tables and get home before it got any darker.

Lucy and Hobo hurriedly started placing the items onto the table. One sock, four felt tip pens, a horseradish...

As they placed the last items onto the table, a low scrape of fingernails on glass distracted them.

'What was that?' Lucy and Hobo said in unison, before rummaging around on the tables. A medium-sized glass jar, complete with lid, lay inside a large upside-down straw hat. Inside the jar was a little creature, clawing away at the sides and trying to make its escape.

'How is it surviving in there? It can't have much air.' Lucy picked up the jar and prised open the lid ever so slightly. As soon as fresh air filled the jar, the little imp calmed down and stopped scratching.

Lucy and Hobo stared at the creature in the jar. It really was the oddest little thing they had ever seen. How it had managed to disguise itself as a rabbit was beyond them. Clutched in the imp's hand was a large cookie.

'Well, I guess we know where the rest of Gran's cookies went,' Hobo said before glancing at the clock on the far wall of the hall. 'We need to get back quickly. Grandad's friends will be here with the food soon and the procession will be starting any minute now.'

Lucy opened up her coat and tucked the glass jar under her armpit before the two friends hurried out of the hall.

Hobo's grandad draped the large cloth over himself until he was completely covered, apart from his black shoes poking out of the bottom, and wandered out of the door into the street. It was getting dark. It had taken quite a while to organise with the village, but the idea had eventually been cleared.

Hobo's gran was locking up the house just as Lucy and Hobo arrived. Everyone was wrapped up warm, apart from Lucy, whose coat was still open. The Mari's skull towered over the parked cars in the street and bobbed along as Hobo's grandad began walking up the slope in the direction of the community hall, the Mari's ribbons flapping in the breeze and the bells tinkling with every step.

Hobo's gran gave Lucy and Hobo a drum each, and Gav had a little bell, which he waved up and down enthusiastically as he followed his grandad up the street, snow crunching underfoot.

'Well, here goes nothing,' Lucy declared, and off they went, keeping a steady rhythm going as they stepped. It took Lucy a little while to get used to carrying the glass jar at the same time as banging on her drum.

Dogs barked and cats meowed as the quintet strolled up the street. Lights were switched on and doors opened around them. People watched from their windows and others, surprisingly, pulled on their shoes and joined their group. Some found it a good excuse to walk their energetic dogs. One man even produced a flute and happily started playing a sweet, melodic tune as he followed the parade.

'Can you hear that?' Hobo asked Lucy. 'The imps are watching.'

Small giggles came in wisps carried by the icy breeze.

'Yes, or they're playing tricks while everyone's backs are turned,' Lucy replied, just as a little giggle sounded from inside the jar.

But the imps weren't the only ones laughing. Gavin thought the whole thing was a lot of fun and began jigging along and laughing to the music. It was infectious.

Soon the group was riled up, chanting, singing and marching to the beat of the drums as they approached the door to the community hall.

The giggles of the imps seemed to get louder.

Just as the Mari reached the door, it opened, revealing a group of people inside. It was time for the Mari to give her rhyme, and the whole party began to sing in Welsh, which Hobo translated as best he could for Lucy.

Here we come
Dear friends.
To ask permissions to sing.
If we don't have permission,
Let us know in song
How we should go away tonight.

After the song ended, the occupants of the community hall came back with rhyming insults, trying their hardest to get rid of the Mari and outwit her in the battle of rhyme and song.

I have no dinner
Or money to spend
To give you welcome tonight.

Hobo tried to keep translating, but after a while even he wasn't sure what was being said. All the songs were sung quickly and with a force that reminded the pair of a real battle.

The imps giggled again, louder. The Mari chanted her song. More rhyming reasons were given for her not to enter. Lucy and Hobo banged on their drums. It seemed to go on for hours. Until finally, the Mari was allowed entry.

The Mari Lwyd passed over the threshold of the building, the party singing quietly as she entered, granting luck on the whole community.

The giggles stopped.

Inside the hall, Hobo's grandad lifted the cloth over his head and placed the Mari to one side, as the entire community filed in through the double doors.

Laid out on tables to the right was enough food and drink to feed an army, and to the left of the room were the piles and piles of lost things. Gavin was the first to notice the piles of stuff.

'My Nintendoooh!' he squealed as he ran across the room. And it wasn't long before everyone else followed.

'Are those my gnomes?' one lady said.

Lucy and Hobo walked over to Hobo's grandad, trying to get out of the way of the crowd. The imp was still in the jar beneath Lucy's coat; she could hear it laughing and munching on the cookie.

'What if it hasn't worked?' Lucy queried.

'Ah, don't you worry. I've arranged a little surprise just to make sure that those pesky things have gone for good.'

Hobo's grandad made his way over to the back entrance of the hall, stood up on a chair and let his voice carry across the whole room. 'Attention, ladies, gentlemen and children, if you would all be so kind as to follow me outside for one final surprise, it would be greatly appreciated.' With a large smile on his face, Hobo's grandad stepped down from the chair and made his way outside.

The community followed, chattering with excitement, and arranged themselves in a semicircle facing the garden.

Hobo's grandad started the chant.

Ten.

Nine.

Eight.

Seven.

Six.

Five.

Four.

Three.

Two.

One.

Fireworks exploded above them in a plethora of colours. Some were loud, some were quiet. Some went in a straight line and some whizzed into the sky in loops. Some crackled, some squealed and some just went bang. Just like heroes – all in different shapes and sizes – they served their purpose in warding off evil spirits.

Lucy took the jar out from beneath her coat. A thin wisp of black smoke swirled out from the air hole in the lid. The imp had simply disappeared and the giggles were long gone.

Hobo looked to his best friend and grinned as he noticed the empty jar. 'Happy New Year, Lucy.'

Lucy grinned back. 'Happy New Year, Hobo. Here's to the future!'

'Which one?'

'What do you mean?'

'Well, it depends if you believe in alternative futures.'

'Shut up, Hobo!'

PAST, PRESENT AND YET TO COME.

Chris Lynch

At the very edge of time and space, where our universe ends and there is nothing but the howling emptiness of the Black Void – that thing that is nothing and yet is the canvas on which our reality is painted – there is a place called 'the Boneyard'.

It is a place where heroes go to die in peace, their victories won and their labours done. There, in the moment between the final tick and the ultimate tock of the clock that measures all time, there is a hope that they might know a small moment of tranquillity and reflect on all the things they have done.

It is the least the universe can do for its heroes.

But 'hero' is a strange word. It can mean a lot of different things.

And some heroes aren't quite so keen to tick tock off like they're supposed to…

The Crone had been in the Boneyard for a long time. Of course 'the Crone' wasn't her real name. The spirits of the Boneyard, the invisible servants who saw to their heroes every need, knew her by many names. They called her the Crone. The Witch. The Woman with Two Faces. The Guardian of the Last Bridge. The Beast of Ogmore. The Terror of Mars. The Anti-General. The Yeti Queen of Ancient Gleet Rigel. Oh yes, they had names for her.

When you're three hundred and eighty-eight

years old, it's hard not to pick up a reputation, and a few good stories.

The spirits liked stories. They were what sustained them. They understood that stories were, and always had been, the building blocks of all reality. From the very first moment that an electron called itself an electron, whizzed around the outside of a thing it named a proton and then began to tell all its friends what it had been up to, the rules of everything had been laid down through the telling of stories.

This is why, you can rest assured, good guys always win.

In the end.

It's also why, with so little time to play with, the spirits had chosen to make the moment in between the last tick and the last tock of the great clock on Christmas Eve. There is no time better for a little nostalgia, a little looking back before all the looking forward of Christmas and the New Year. There's also no better time for a good ghost story. Ghosts from the past, ghosts from the present, and ghosts from the future were welcomed, one and all.

The Crone had come to hate Christmas, and although she had met ghosts on more than one occasion, she curiously still refused to really believe in them. Perhaps if she had, she might have been a little scared the day a boy who by now would have been long dead visited the Boneyard in a magic box that could fly through space and time.

The Crone woke up as she always did, right at the tick. Time in the Boneyard was a loop, jumping backwards to the last tick in the fraction of a fraction of a split-moment before the last tock was heard. Everyone remembered what they had been doing, but everything else reset itself, and everyone woke up once more, just as they had done on their very first day in the Boneyard.

The only thing that ever seemed to change was just how long there was between the tick and the tock. Sometimes there was barely enough time to sit up in bed, other times days would go by before the Boneyard and its inhabitants were catapulted back up the timestream.

Mad Old Jackson swore blind that he'd once experienced eighteen years, four months, three weeks and two days between the tick and the tock. Nobody believed him, of course. When you go around with a name like 'Mad Old Jackson'.

For simplicity, and to avoid arguments with Mad Old Jackson, all the inhabitants of the Boneyard just called however much time they had 'a day'. A day that was forever Christmas Eve.

The Crone needed her staff to walk at any great speed, which is why she kept it by the bed. It was a simple shaft of gnarled old wood, a metal band around its middle, and the Crone guarded it fiercely, as it was the only real possession that she had. Leaning on it, she made her way from the small but comfortable bed that the spirits afforded her to the small but functional bathroom.

Each person's quarters in the Boneyard were styled to their personal tastes. Some were lavish, some were homely. Some, in keeping with the beliefs of their inhabitants, were modelled after the afterlife that person had always expected they would have. There were more than a few hells, as a consequence. 'Hero' is a funny word, after all, and the spirits of the Boneyard could be quite mischievous in their interpretation of what a 'moment of quiet reflection' fully entailed. Some people do their best thinking under the strangest of circumstances.

The Crone's quarters were exceptionally Spartan. A bed. A chair. A bookcase (empty). A desk (bare except for an unfinished Rubik's cube). One window, curtains drawn and never opened. The walls and floor were bare, as if neither art nor carpets had ever been invented.

The bathroom, at least, had the usual fixtures and fittings, all in a dull brushed chrome. If the decor had a name it would have been 'low tech military', although the Crone herself gave off an air that made it clear she was the type of person who did not fit well into structures or hierarchy. This was perhaps why the spirits had made her quarters such a blank canvas; they didn't really know what to do with her. Or perhaps it was because the Crone didn't naturally take to tranquillity and spent most days, if they proved long enough, testing the security of the Boneyard with repeated escape attempts.

Leaning on her staff in the bathroom the Crone stared into the mirror, a much older woman than she remembered ever being looked back at her. A fringe benefit of living backwards and forwards at the edge of time was that you didn't age, which was for the best as the Crone didn't look as if she had one more day left in her. Her hair, once dark, was now a mad frenzy of silver and grey. It hung down over one side of her face, covering the eye patch that sat over her left eye and the deep scar that knew the story of how she lost it. Her dark skin was patterned with wrinkles to go with the scars, a complex map of a long life that had seen more than its fair share of danger and death. She smiled a crooked smile, examining her teeth, glad to see that they, at least, were all still there. She wasn't allowed a toothbrush anymore; she guessed the spirits must somehow clean her teeth when she slept. She didn't like that.

Today felt like a good day to escape from the end of everything.

However, there was one thing that was different

in the mirror this morning, which of course should have been impossible. It took the Crone a moment to notice it, mostly because it couldn't possibly have been there.

But it was.

There was a boy in the mirror.

The Crone spun around, whipping her staff up from the floor and bringing the tip up fast under the boy's chin. It stopped less than a centimetre from the boy's throat, quivering in the air with violent potential.

'Hello, Lucy,' said the boy, swallowing nervously. 'It's good to see you?'

'Who the hell is Lucy?'

'Lima Bravo, this is Umbrella, what's your status?'

Major Lethbridge-Stewart peeked out of cover, then quickly ducked back in again.

'Well, I can confirm the presence of an absolutely massive and terrifying spaceship over London, does that count?'

'Say again, Lima Bravo?

The major sighed. 'Contact confirmed. I have eyes on the target.'

'Roger that, Lima Bravo.'

The spaceship was indeed massive and terrifying. Office blocks rose up on every side of the major's vantage point on the deserted London street, and what little sky they didn't obscure was blocked entirely by the underside of the ship. Adjusting the goggles built into her helmet, the major studied it carefully.

'Umbrella, do you copy?'

'Go ahead, Lima Bravo.'

'I'm seeing at least twelve different alien technologies on this thing, only a few I recognise.'

'I make it... seventeen.'

'Who is this?' asked the voice of Umbrella urgently. 'Please identify yourself.'

The major closed her eyes for just a second and offered up a silent prayer. When aliens turned up, when there was a very good chance that your entire planet was about to be ransacked, enslaved, burnt to ash or worse, there was really only one person you wanted to hear from. The stupid helmets made everyone's voice sound the same, and so she prayed it was him.

'Hotel Kilo, also on site.'

The major breathed a sigh of relief.

'Thought you couldn't make it, Hobo?'

'Got a lift off a friend.'

Major Lucy Lethbridge-Stewart grinned. Those aliens? They were in real trouble now.

'Lucy, it's me?' said the boy incredulously. 'It's Hobo.'

The Crone looked at the-boy-who-called-himself-Hobo, her one good eye moving slowly over every inch of him like a predator stalking a herd.

'No,' she said gruffly. 'Still don't know you.'

Hobo took a step backward. Barely fourteen, he had the height and bulk of a much older boy. He was dressed in jeans and a plain, dark hoodie. His head was completely bald and his eyebrows missing, alopecia having robbed him of his hair. The Crone took a step forward, keeping her staff at Hobo's throat.

'You're different,' she croaked. 'Unusual.'

'I get that a lot. I did try a wig once, remember?'

'Not that. I mean you weren't here yesterday.'

'No, I just arrived.'

'There are never new people,' said the Crone. 'Not here.'

That was one of the other things about the Boneyard; everyone seemed to have been here from the beginning, from the very first last tick.

'Well, I'm here,' replied Hobo. 'So, now there are. Things are only impossible until somebody does them.'

The Crone smiled. 'Well then, Mr Hobo, let's see if you can manage two impossible things before breakfast, shall we?"

The Crone lowered her staff and shuffled off towards the door.

'I'll lead, you follow.'

'Typical Lucy move,' said Hobo.

It took Hobo and Major Lucy Lethbridge-Stewart eight minutes to climb the stairs to the top of the office block, find the access ladder and clamber up to the roof. For Lucy it was a new personal best, whereas Hobo had barely broken a sweat.

'Don't you train?' asked Hobo, waiting for Lucy to catch her breath.

'Not as much… as you… clearly…' replied Lucy, pulling off her helmet and dropping it to the ground. Her Umbrella uniform felt heavy, with too much equipment in her pockets, and strapped to her belt and across her back.

Hobo flipped up his helmet visor. Still no eyebrows, Lucy noticed, but the same kind eyes regardless.

'You need to train, Lucy. You can't get by on gut instinct and luck forever, you know.'

Lucy straightened up, taking one last deep lungful of air.

'You've literally been telling me that for a decade, Hobo. You're going to have to admit defeat eventually.'

Hobo looked up at the ship overhead. It stretched as far as they could see in every direction, a ramshackle combination of technologies that blended into and overlapped one another. As they watched, a ripple passed over the surface of the thing, reconfiguring and replacing and changing the arrangement of the mismatched machinery.

'Let's see how we get on today,' said Hobo grimly. 'Live through this one, and I just might concede.'

'What's it doing?' asked Lucy. 'It's changing.'

'Evolving?' suggested Hobo. 'Adapting? Whatever it's doing it's probably not good for us.'

'When is it ever?'

'Fair point,' replied Hobo. He unsnapped a cylinder from the back of his belt and began twisting a large dial on one side.

'I see you got an extra stripe,' said Lucy, poking the Umbrella rank insignia on Hobo's shoulder.

'Yeah,' said Hobo, unable to hide some small amount of pride in his promotion.

'After the Tokyo mission. Feels right, you know?

Lucy smiled earnestly at her friend. She'd always believed he'd run the country one day; now he was on his way to running the world. 'I'll be calling you Brigadier soon.'

'The Umbrella's getting bigger, Lucy. It needs good people at the top. It needs you.'

'I'm happy as I am, Hobo,' replied Lucy, pulling a matching cylinder from the back of her belt. 'I was born into this thing, I didn't choose it. I've seen what it does to people, in the end.'

Lucy glanced down at Hobo's cylinder.

'Twenty-eight.'

'What?'

'Turn the dial to twenty-eight, Lucy.'

Lucy twisted the dial on her cylinder. 'Thanks.'

'You really don't train at all, do you?' Hobo raised his arm, aiming his cylinder at the underside of the vast ship that hung motionless above them. Lucy did the same.

'Wait, we'll go after the next ripple,' said Lucy.

'You're sure?'

'Gut instinct.'

Hobo rolled his eyes. 'Well, it's got us this far.'

Another ripple passed overhead, the configuration of the ship changing again.

Lucy squeezed the cylinder tight and, with a sudden pop and cloud of white gas, a metal cable burst out and flew up towards the underside of the alien ship. Hobo squeezed his too, a second cable snaking up after the first. The cables hit home and, a second later, the cylinders let out a high pitched whine and both Lucy and Hobo were hoisted up into the air, heading towards the ship.

'Is this the biggest ship we've ever broken into?' shouted Lucy, the sound of rushing air and the whine of her grapple filling her ears.

'Yeah, I think so,' Hobo called back, his eyes fixed on the vessel above.

'Cool,' said Lucy. 'Cool.'

The door of the Crone's room led out onto the main atrium, just like every door of every other room in the Boneyard. 'Atrium', however, was somewhat too small a word for what the place actually was. The atrium was so vast that it was impossible to see from one side to the other; where you would have expected the other side of the room to be there was a horizon, and where you would have expected the corner of the room to be there was just the slightest curve as the wall bent inwards. Every few feet there was a door, the gateway to one of the Boneyard's inhabitants personalised spaces. As for the atrium itself, it was a pristine white space interspersed with a seemingly endless array of chairs, sofas, occasional tables, cushions, rugs, pots of steaming tea and plates of biscuits. Everything was bedecked in Christmas paraphernalia and there were more Christmas trees than had ever grown in all of time.

The easiest way to imagine what the atrium felt like was to imagine a planet turned inside out and then filled with the contents of every grandmother's living room ever from all of history, all trapped like air in a balloon.

Above them, the ceiling was entirely dominated

by a single giant clock. It had just two numbers, a one and a zero, and a single hand that was moving slowly from the one down to the zero. No matter where you stood in the atrium, you could always see the clock, counting slowly down. The hand was moving quickly today. It would be a short day.

Thankfully, it wasn't far to Hobo's spaceship.

'What... is... that?' asked the Crone.

'My ship,' replied Hobo nervously. 'Well, not mine exactly. I had to borrow it.'

The Crone turned and fixed Hobo with a withering stare. If she'd had two eyes, she could probably have turned him to stone where he stood.

'It's a box,' she said sharply.

'It's not just a box,' said Hobo defensively. 'It's a Punch and Judy box.'

The Crone pushed past Hobo and headed back towards the door to her room.

'You're wasting my time,' she said bitterly. 'Which is saying something, given that it's been Christmas Eve here forever.'

'Lucy, wait!' called Hobo. 'Please!'

The Crone stopped, halfway between the atrium and her room.

'I'm not Lucy,' she growled. 'I don't know you.'

'Then ask me!' shouted Hobo. His whole body was shaking and he could feel tears like pinpricks at the backs of his eyes. He forced his trembling hands into the pockets of his hoodie and twisted the material tight between his fingers.

'Ask me, please. Ask me because… because I've come right across time and space in a box, a very small box I might add, looking for you. Earth is in danger, real danger, and I need help! I need help so much that I asked anyone, and everyone, right across the whole universe and only one person answered. One person gave me a chance and the chance that they gave me is you!'

The Crone tightened her grip on her staff.

'Earth,' she whispered.

'Please,' said Hobo desperately.

The Crone turned once more and if Hobo's eyes hadn't been dewy with tears he might have noticed that, somehow, the Crone looked suddenly a little younger. A light, a spark, somewhere deep inside, had been rekindled. If even half the stories about the Crone were true, lighting that spark meant that you should, immediately, stand well back.

The Crone stamped her staff on the ground, a loud snap that echoed back from across the atrium.

'Are you clever?' asked the Crone. 'You look clever.'

Hobo wiped his eyes on the sleeve of his hoodie.

'I'm a fourteen-year-old boy who just flew a puppet show to the edge of reality.'

The Crone banged her staff on the floor again.

The echo came back, quicker this time than before.

'Then tell me something,' asked the Crone. 'We're standing in a room so large that we can't see the other side of it.' She slammed her staff once more on to the hard floor, cocking her head as the echo came back. 'So, where's that echo coming from?'

Hobo didn't have time to answer as, in the distance, something began moving rapidly towards them with a sound like grating chains. Chairs flew up into the air, tables toppled, all knocked aside by the invisible force.

'What is it?' asked Hobo.

'The spirits,' answered the Crone. 'The things that run this place.'

The sound of clanking, clinking, grating chains got closer as more furniture was tossed up into the air, landing with a crash in the distance. An invisible wave of force was approaching, knocking aside everything in its path.

'And why, exactly, did you let them know we were here?' said Hobo, a note of panic in his voice.

The Crone grinned. 'Testing a theory. Plus, I needed to know if you were one of them.'

Suddenly, something invisible snaked around Hobo's legs and dragged him down to the floor. He landed hard on his front and was dragged quickly backward, away from the Crone and from his ship. He reached out, trying to get hold of anything he could.

The rattling and clanking grew louder as a door flew open in the wall. Beyond it, the howling nothingness of the Black Void waited.

'Lucy, help!' screamed Hobo.

The Crone shrugged. 'Okay, so not one of them,' she said to herself. 'Look like it's game on then.' She stuck two fingers into her mouth and whistled.

A door burst open in the wall and out of it came tumbling the largest man that Hobo had ever seen. Eight or nine feet tall, five feet wide at the shoulder, with hands the size of car tyres. He was dressed in what looked like an enormous Victorian nightshirt, although it was possibly just the sails of a ship that had been stitched together. He had a huge red beard that hung down almost to his waist and a mass of bright red curly hair on top of his head.

The giant looked at Hobo, then at the Crone, then at Hobo again.

'Is it Christmas?' he asked.

'Afraid not, Jackson,' replied the Crone. 'But if you wouldn't mind…'

The Crone nodded in the direction of Hobo, who was still skidding across the atrium floor. Jackson took two colossal steps, catching up with Hobo in an instant, and scooped him up by the scruff of the neck. The invisible things held onto Hobo's leg tight, and Jackson shook him in mid-air to get them to let go.

'Get out of it!' he bellowed, and with a clank and a clatter the spirits moved off. They circled around in a pack, stalking their prey.

Jackson tossed Hobo through the air and he landed in a heap at the Crone's feet. Nursing his one ankle, Hobo looked around, trying to pin down the source of the constant clanking of chains.

'What are they?' he asked.

'Stories,' replied the Crone. 'Histories. Reputation. Choices that were made and chances never taken. The chains we make in life...'

Hobo furrowed his brow. 'That sounds familiar.'

The ventilation grate in the floor of the ship popped open, allowing Lucy and Hobo to clamber up. Lucy scanned the corridor in both directions while Hobo carefully replaced the grate.

'You know,' said Lucy. 'If aliens ever figure out what a massive security risk ventilation shafts are, we're going to be in trouble.'

A ripple ran down the corridor, transforming everything around them. The corridor got narrower and the grating disappeared.

'Interesting,' said Hobo, crouching down to examine the patch of floor where the grating had been. 'Like it was never there.'

Lucy shook her head. 'I really need to stop

thinking out loud.'

'I don't think it was you, exactly,' said Hobo. 'But have you noticed how each time the ship changes, it gets a little more advanced?'

'Oh yeah,' said Lucy, 'absolutely. Like these, err, these things…'

Lucy waved her hand around in no direction in particular.

Hobo sighed.

'Okay, honestly, I lost track of what tech, whoever these guys are, have got about four or five changes ago. It's like this ship doesn't really exist or something.'

'Or something,' replied Hobo.

Lucy looked up and down the corridor again.

'This way,' she said, turning away from Hobo and heading off down the corridor.

'You're sure?'

Lucy tapped a finger to the side of her head. 'Lethbridge-Stewart radar. Always points directly towards danger and trouble – definitely this way.'

Hobo got up and followed Lucy. Danger and trouble pretty much summed her up.

The Punch and Judy show unfolded itself into existence in the car park of Ogmore sea front. It was a particular part of the way that it worked that nobody would notice, except for the appearance of a few tatty fliers advertising the puppet show that simultaneously appeared on nearby lamp-posts.

Hobo popped out of the back of the box, forcibly ejected by the Crone.

He staggered a few paces, then straightened up, holding his hand against the small of his back.

'Must have... got taller since last time,' he muttered to himself.

The Crone stepped out, leaning on her staff once more. She took the sea air in great lungfuls and looked around with a strange smile on her lips.

Hobo turned. 'Welcome to Ogmore-by-Sea,' he said. 'Population... dwindling.'

'Ogmore,' said the Crone wistfully. 'That's a name I haven't heard in a very long time.'

'So you do remember!' said Hobo. 'I knew it.'

The Crone didn't answer, patting the side of the Punch and Judy box as she hobbled away up the car park.

'Nice little ride,' she called back over her shoulder, changing the subject. 'Now, tell me about this... dwindling.'

Lucy and Hobo stopped at a junction between two corridors as the ship reconfigured itself around them. When the ripple had passed by, the junction was gone and they were facing a dead end.

'Think it's a defence mechanism?' said Hobo,

pressing his hand against the new wall that appeared in front of them. 'Keeping us trapped?'

Lucy looked around, checking the floors, the walls, the ceiling.

'No,' she said. 'I think you were right the first time – this tech is just a little more advanced than before. It's not defending itself, it's evolving.'

'Evolving?'

'Yeah. Right now, let's say we're standing in ship version 1.0. The wave comes through and changes things, that's version 1.1. And it keeps happening, faster and faster…'

'Until?'

'No idea,' said Lucy. 'But I do have a theory.'

Lucy pulled two cylinders off her belt, one from the left and one from the right, and snapped them together. With a twist, they lit up.

'Whoa, whoa!' said Hobo. 'You know the blast radius on that?'

'Worried you can't outrun it, Mr "You need to train more"?'

'Worried about the somewhat important city right underneath us is more like it.'

'Don't worry,' said Lucy, holding the bomb against the wall, where it attached with a magnetic clang. 'If I'm right, it's never going off.'

'And if you're wrong?'

'Well, I don't want to live in a world where that's

a possibility, do you?'

The bomb bleeped. Ten seconds.

Nine.

Eight.

A ripple passed through, subtly changing the corridor around them again. Suddenly, Lucy and Hobo were in a room without doors. No way out. Lights blinked in the wall behind the bomb, pulsing in time with the countdown.

Six.

Five.

Four.

'Lucy?'

Three.

Two.

One.

Another ripple passed through the room. The bomb disappeared, swallowed up by the wall it had been attached to just as the wall itself receded, the tiny room-without-doors expanding into something much larger.

Lucy and Hobo spun around. The room had opened up into a large, circular space now. Shadows danced on the walls, cast by unseen lights. Shapes morphing and changing as the ship did, until one shadow peeled itself away from the wall on freshly formed legs and walked, awkwardly at first, towards Hobo and Lucy.

Arms sprouted from the torso, stretching down to where the shadow had tapered itself a waist. A head, little more than a dark, flat egg at first, bubbled up from the torso. It inclined itself left and right, regarding Lucy and Hobo with eyes that simply were not there.

The egg split open, forming a mouth that was far too big and that curved upwards into a smile that was nothing like a smile at all.

'Lucy,' whispered Hobo, 'What did you do?'

'I got someone's attention.'

Two more slits appeared in the egg, opening up where eyes should have been, showing nothing but the wall behind the creature. Watching Lucy and Hobo with its empty eyes, the thing spoke from its empty mouth.

'Hello,' it said.

'Hello,' replied Lucy. She took a step forward, pulling off her tactical gloves before reaching out one hand. 'My name is Lucy and, well, you're on my planet.'

The shadow-thing inclined its head, folding it over like a piece of paper, the eye slits popping open into circle shapes. It stared at Lucy's hand.

'It's a greeting,' explained Lucy. 'You take my hand in yours.'

The creature straightened its head and the too wide smile turned into a frown.

'We are unaware of your protocol,' said the shadow-thing. 'This is non-optimal.'

A ripple ran through the room and, without warning, the ship pitched forwards. Hobo and Lucy lost their footing for a moment as the interior of the ship changed once again, the clean metal plating and elegant technology giving way to rusted plates, heavy pipes, and exposed wiring that sparked and fizzed.

The shadow-thing looked left and right, its eyes moving in two different directions at the same time.

'What happened?' asked Lucy.

'We were unaware of your protocol,' answered the shadow-thing. Its face achieved more definition as its eyes came back together, its mouth achieving more regular proportions. 'We are now aware. We have optimised.'

'I meant your ship,' said Lucy, lurching into Hobo as the ship pitched to the side for the second time.

'We optimised,' replied the shadow-thing. 'There are consequences, sometimes.'

Hobo followed the Crone up the road towards Ogmore itself. For an old lady from the end of time, she set quite a pace.

'How many did you say again?' she asked over her shoulder.

'Thirteen,' replied Hobo. 'That I know of. There might have been others, people I didn't know. Lucy was last... that was when I started to ask for help.'

The Crone grunted something under her breath before asking, 'And they just disappear?'

'Not exactly,' replied Hobo. 'They do disappear but it's not just like they are there one day and gone the next. It's like they were never there, ever. Like they've been erased from the world and from people's memories at the same time.'

'But you remember them?' asked the Crone.

'Yes,' said Hobo, finally catching up. 'Don't ask me why but... I remember them.'

'And the things you remember,' asked the Crone, 'how can you be sure that they're real?'

'What do you mean?' asked Hobo.

The Crone stopped. 'I mean,' she said, 'if a person only exists in your head, if you have no physical evidence of them ever having had existed... how can you be sure that they were ever real at all?'

'I'm not mad,' said Hobo defensively. 'I'm not. I guard my mind.'

'Guard your mind,' mused the Crone. 'Hmm.'

'I know you're her,' said Hobo. 'You have to be.'

The Crone rolled her eyes. 'And why's that? Because whoever loaned you that box told you so?'

'No,' replied Hobo, looking down at his feet. 'Because the last person to disappear was Lucy. And if you're not her then, well… she's really gone.'

Lucy and Hobo collided with each other as the ship pitched backwards. The ship's hull creaked and groaned like a dying animal.

'We're falling, aren't we?' gasped Lucy.

'I'd say so.'

The shadow creature looked around, its empty eyes passing over the interior of the ship. It moved, not walking but somehow extending and contracting its legs like pistons, and placed the pointed tip of one arm onto the wall.

A ripple ran through the walls again, larger than any that Lucy or Hobo had seen before, a visible bending of the world that sent a stale wind across the room. Behind the ripple came another new version of the ship, a gleaming white version that shone with a strange and otherworldly light.

The ship suddenly levelled out. Lucy and Hobo tumbled to the floor together, quickly righting themselves before the creature turned back from the freshly recreated wall.

Hobo kept one hand on the floor.

'What is it?' whispered Lucy.

'Feels different,' replied Hobo under his breath. 'Different engine.'

Lucy looked around. 'Different ship,' she replied.

The shadow-thing turned, rotating its head

completely then reversing its approximations of arms and legs. Walking on the tips of its pointed legs, it advanced on Lucy and Hobo, a smile once more splitting open its oval head.

It reached out, its arm ending in a pointed tip. 'It's a greeting,' said the creature. 'You take my hand in yours.'

Lucy watched as fingers like scissor blades extruded themselves from the tip of the inky black arm. She swallowed her nerves and reached out her own hand.

'I wouldn't do that,' said Hobo, grabbing Lucy by the forearm. He was holding a small scanning unit in his free hand, one of Umbrella's toys that Lucy would have probably taken the time to understand if she didn't have such unshakeable faith in her own intuition.

Lucy's hand hovered in mid-air, inches from the scissor-tip fingers of the creature.

'It is a greeting,' said the creature, its voice becoming stern.

Hobo held the scanner up so that Lucy could see the display.

'It's not there,' he said. 'That's not an alien. It's some sort of negative space... it would be like touching a black hole.'

Lucy yanked her hand back. The creature that wasn't a creature, the shadow that wasn't a shadow, dropped its head to look down at Lucy and Hobo.

'It was a greeting.'

'Let's just say hello, shall we?' said Lucy.

The creature seemed to stare at Lucy for a moment, the empty voids in its head occupied by a view of the glowing white walls of the ship. Then it twisted its head to stare at Hobo.

'Lucy… I don't like this,' said Hobo. He took a step back, his hand moving to the pouches on his belt. Lucy never found out what he was reaching for. In a flash, the blade-like tips of the creature's fingers sliced through the air and vanished inside Hobo. There was a ripple, emanating from Hobo's chest as if he were nothing more than a picture painted on the surface of a lake.

Hobo Kostinen dissolved to nothingness, torn silently and gently asunder by the ripple that passed through the air like a breeze over water.

'Hobo!' Lucy screamed.

But it was too late.

Hobo was gone.

The Crone lumbered past Ogmore's small run of seaside shops, curling her lip at the range of plastic buckets, spades, beach balls, and small inflatable boats.

'I'd forgotten these existed,' she grumbled.

'I didn't bring you here to make sandcastles,' said

Hobo irritably.

'Don't worry,' said the Crone, tapping the side of her nose. 'I've got a special sense for danger and it never lets me down. If I just wait here long enough…'

The Crone twirled a spinner rack of novelty key rings, stopping it in the 'L' section and picking out a plastic cat with the name 'Lucy' on it.

'Any minute now…'

Hobo was about to let out an exasperated sigh when, right on cue, there was a scream from inside the shop.

'Ah,' said the Crone, sounding slightly relieved. 'There we go.'

Lucy staggered back from the space where Hobo had been standing a moment before. A pale outline of him hovered in place for a moment, before fading away, leaving no trace of the man who had been Lucy's best friend since childhood.

That was it. Their game, their great adventure, their endless rounds of chicken with the best and worst of the universe combined was over. Lucy wondered how she had thought it might end. Hadn't this been inevitable, somehow? One of them had to fall, eventually.

Lucy decided it didn't matter. Hobo was gone, that was all there was to it, and the space that he had once occupied was now filled with nothing but a white hot fury. The fury of Lucy Lethbridge-Stewart. Had the stars known, they would have trembled in their orbits.

Lucy turned to face the creature, the shadow-thing with scissor -fingers, her face contorted by rage.

'What did you do?'

'We optimised,' replied the creature. 'Your actions here could not be predicted. Our first optimisation was flawed and we briefly lost our engines. This new optimisation is a great improvement, but your friend is... unnecessary.'

'Unnecessary?' snarled Lucy. 'Unnecessary?!'

She fumbled with the pouches on her belt, pulling another cylinder like the one she had attached to the ship, just minutes before.

'You will not come here and take my people,' she said, her voice shaking slightly. 'You are not the first to try and, oh, you're the first to manage it, all right – so, yeah, take some pride in that – but you will be the last.'

'We do not understand,' replied the creature. Its empty eyes were drawn to the cylinder in Lucy's hand. She twisted it, hard, and a bright red ring illuminated.

'They've had me on a leash, you know? The great big mighty Umbrella, protecting the whole world from rainy alien days. Well, maybe if we'd taken that umbrella and shoved it where the sun doesn't shine with the first lot of you that came here…'

'Ahhh,' said the creature. 'We see. It is you that does not understand.'

And, with that, the creature thrust its ebon fingers into Lucy's chest.

The Crone crashed into the gift shop, the door bouncing off the wall. A little bell tinkled overhead. It wasn't the entrance she wanted to make, but it would have to do.

Behind the shop counter, a young girl was screaming as a black figure stood over her. A black figure with a head shaped like an egg, long, pointed fingers, and empty voids where eyes should be.

'You…' said the Crone.

'You…' replied the creature, freezing where it stood.

Out of the corner of her good eye the Crone could see Hobo creeping, head down, past a display of Ogmore snow globes, beckoning the young girl from behind the counter to make a break for safety.

'It begins here,' replied the creature. 'There will be consequences.'

The girl, petrified with fright, refused to move. The Crone motioned for Hobo to stay where he was. She didn't want him any closer to the creature.

'Let the girl go,' said the Crone. 'Or I'll show you

some consequences.'

The girl let out another scream. Hobo, ignoring the Crone's subtle instruction, lunged forward to grab her. The creature, its dagger fingers extruding, made ready to claim its victim.

'Okay, here we go,' growled the Crone. She held her staff aloft, then brought it down hard across her knee. It split in two, the metal ring that had run around the middle of it spinning up into the air. The Crone caught it deftly and slipped the ring onto her finger.

Hobo gasped. 'That's Lucy's ring...'

The Crone held her hand, palm up, to the creature. 'Go.'

A white light filled the room for a moment, so bright that Hobo had to shield his eyes. When he could see again, the creature was gone. The girl from behind the counter finally found her legs, and vanished out of the shop.

'We should go,' said the Crone. 'Your mother will be coming through the door in a few minutes.'

'My mother?' asked Hobo.

'She's still a police officer, isn't she?'

'I knew it was you, Lucy,' said Hobo with a wide grin. His eyes were shining, with tears or excitement it was impossible to say. 'Why were you pretending?'

'I had my reasons,' said the Crone. She glared at the spot where the shadow creature had been.

'Reasons that may be about to change.'

Lucy opened her eyes and found herself standing on the lawn of the small sunlit garden of a red brick cottage. A gentle breeze tickled the leaves of a few small trees and flowerbeds that were just coming into bloom. The smell of spring was in the air, a far cry from the strange and stale air of the vessel she had been standing in moments before.

The shadow creature stood next to her and she noticed immediately that neither it, nor she, cast a shadow on the ground.

'Where are we?' she asked.

'We call it The Interface,' replied the creature. 'From here, we can optimise.'

Lucy thought the thing looked more real here, more three dimensional, until she realised with a start that it was in fact her that had flattened out. She turned her hand back and forth in front of her face, marvelling at the strange elongated flatness of it. Her fingertips brushed something in front of her, something invisible that felt like ice cold water. The world beyond the Interface rippled, the same way that the ship had rippled around her. The way it had rippled around Hobo.

'Have a care,' said the creature. 'The Interface is delicate.'

Suddenly the back door of the red brick cottage

burst open and a gaggle of children came piling out. Three, four, then five, they ran and shouted and tripped and laughed until they finally collapsed in a wrestling, play-fighting heap in the middle of the lawn. Three boys, two girls. One boy completely bald, one of the girls with skin the brightest blue Lucy had ever seen.

Then, another figure at the door. A figure that made Lucy gasp.

'Hobo,' she said in a whisper, her voice catching in her throat. 'Hobo!'

Hobo, this new Hobo, limped out of the door. In one hand he balanced a tray full of glasses of lemonade, with the other he kept his weight steady with a metal cane. He walked awkwardly, his left leg unable to bend or take much weight. He was a little older, by Lucy's estimations, or maybe just out of shape. He was still hairless, but his face was more careworn and his shoulders slouched a little. The world, perhaps, had ground him down just a bit.

'Kids!' he called out. 'I've got… woah!'

Hobo's cane punctured the ground, dipping a few inches down some invisible hole in the lawn. It wasn't much, but it was enough to make him trip and fall face first onto the lawn, the tray of lemonade crashing down with him.

The children immediately gave up their game and came running to help.

One of the girls, the one with blue skin, who seemed a little older or maybe just a little more mature than the rest, struggled to help Hobo to his feet.

'It's all right, it's all right,' said this new Hobo, irritation in his voice betraying his wounded pride. 'Just be careful of the glass, Ylime.'

The girl, Ylime, must have been stronger than she looked because she hoisted Hobo to his feet with ease and, once his cane was restored, busied herself clearing up the tray and glasses. Hobo hobbled over to an old deck chair and gingerly set himself down in it.

One of the boys wandered over as the others, Ylime included, got back to their game of 'who will be going to casualty first and whose fault will it be' (a modern variation of the game 'you'll have someone's eye out with that', which was adapted from the early prototype 'this will end in tears').

'It's okay, Papa,' he said. 'It's only lemonade.'

Hobo ruffled the boy's hair. 'It's all right, Casper. Just one of those times, you know?'

Casper looked away, his lip trembling. 'One of those times when you miss Mummy?' he asked, his voice quavering.

Hobo gave a sad smile. 'Yeah,' he said. 'One of those times.'

With a groan he pushed himself back up to his

feet on his cane. 'Come on, little soldier,' he said to the boy. 'I'll make some more lemonade and this time you can carry it.

The boy snapped off a reasonable approximation of a salute and together the two of them headed back inside, leaving the rest of the children to continue their game.

'What am I seeing?' asked Lucy. 'What is this?'

'This is your friend,' replied the shadow creature. 'We have optimised him.'

'Optimised...' said Lucy, slowly bending her mind around the concept. 'This is really him now? This is real?'

'Yes,' replied the creature. There was something in its voice that Lucy couldn't place. Compassion? Pride maybe? 'Can you not see what an improvement this is? He is safe, he has family.'

'I was his family,' said Lucy, venom dripping from every word. 'You've crippled him and broken his heart.'

'Optimisation often has consequences.'

'How long?' asked Lucy, staring up into the blank face of the shadow creature. 'How long have you been doing this?'

'Always,' replied the creature. 'We have always been doing this. Optimisation is... gradual. Eventual. Inevitable.'

'And is this what it looks like?' said Lucy,

incredulous. 'Snatching people out of the world and dropping them off in a different life? Changing things willy-nilly to suit yourselves?'

'We improve things,' implored the creature. 'We optimise.'

'And what about me? What about the people who knew Hobo? Do we just forget, is that it? What about all the things he did, the things we did? You have no idea the lives that man has saved, how many times he saved me!'

The creature shook its head slowly. 'You do not understand. You will forget. The life he led is gone and this new, better life takes its place. He has children. He has a place in the world.'

'And the people he saved? The worlds he saved?'

'Consequences,' replied the creature. 'But we will optimise them also. All will be optimised. The universe will be optimised.'

'For you,' said Lucy quietly. 'You mean the universe will be optimised for you.'

Without another word, without a moment's hesitation, Lucy shoved her hand forward again through the icy barrier of the Interface. Passing through it completely, she watched as it transformed into the black, scissor-fingered hand of a shadow creature... except for one thing. There, sitting proudly on the pointed finger of her jet black hand, was Lucy's silver ring.

The ring she had been given long ago, during her first encounter with alien life, by a member of her strange extended family. The ring that was so much more than a ring. The ring that had saved her life maybe even more times than Hobo Kostinen.

'Ha,' said Lucy. 'Didn't count on my bling, did you?'

The creature's eyes opened from slits to wide open circles. Here, on this side of the Interface, there was nothing to show. There was only the void, the great black void, a place where things that didn't exist howled and raged against their nothingness.

'You're not from around here, are you?' asked Lucy. 'Hobo nailed it. He said you weren't there. That's the point isn't it? You're not there. You're not there because you're not supposed to be and you need to change things in our universe until it's just right for you.'

Pulling her hand back through the interface, Lucy grabbed a hold of the creature. Her ring blazed on her finger, incandescent with a white light.

'What happens if I shove you through there, eh? If I become one of you when I go through, what happens to you?'

The creature's mouth sprang open, a gnashing nest of razor sharp teeth.

'You cannot!' it screamed. 'We are not ready! We are not yet optimal!'

Lucy swung her leg around and used her boot to press the creature forward. It squirmed and writhed, bending itself impossibly, but Lucy's grip, and Lucy's ring, held it firm. The smooth blackness of the thing degraded as it got closer to the invisible surface of the Interface, breaking apart into millions of tiny, writhing worm-like things.

Lucy pushed, the thing pushed back, the ring blazed with light.

'Tell me...' snarled Lucy. 'How many people are dead now because of what you did?'

'All things die,' replied the creature. 'To die is optimal.'

'You first then,' said Lucy, and shoved the creature forward through the Interface.

'Where are you going now?' called Hobo, chasing the Crone once more along Ogmore beach.

'Back to the ship,' growled the old woman. She wasn't as steady on her feet without her staff; the fishing net on a long pole that she'd liberated from the gift shop wasn't as good a replacement as she had hoped it might be.

'That's it?' said Hobo. 'What about the people that thing took?'

'Gone,' replied the Crone. 'To better places, if you believe that nonsense.'

Hobo stopped, his breath leaving his chest and

refusing to come back.

'Lucy's... dead?'

The Crone stopped too, turning back to face Hobo. He had slumped down to the ground, sitting with his knees tucked up under his chin, the hood of his hoodie pulled up over his head.

'Hey!' she called.

'Leave me alone,' said Hobo, his voice ragged and choking.

'Hey!' she called again

Hobo yanked his hoodie back off his head. His eyes were red, his cheeks streaked with tears.

'If Lucy's dead, then who the hell am I?' she asked

Hobo wiped his eyes on the sleeve of his hoodie. 'I don't know.'

'A few minutes ago you were convinced I was Lucy. Now, what? I'm suddenly out of the possible-Lucy-future club?'

Hobo shook his head. He didn't know what to think anymore. Boys from Ogmore weren't supposed to go travelling from one end of the universe to the other in wooden boxes. Boys from Ogmore weren't supposed to fight shadow creatures, or monsters, or aliens. He had always prided himself on being the smart one, the clever one, the brains to balance Lucy's gut instinct and weird knack for all things cosmic and strange, but now... now he was just a kid and he was out of his depth.

'Hey!'

'I don't know, okay?' replied Hobo sullenly. 'You said she was gone.

The Crone limped back, a lopsided smile on her scarred old face, and sat down clumsily next to Hobo.

'Oh, Hobo,' she said gently, her voice the softest it had been in a long, long time. 'I said gone, not dead. Gone is just… gone.'

'What's the difference?' sniffed Hobo.

'The difference?' said the Crone with a chuckle. 'The difference is we've got a time machine.'

Hobo looked at the old woman. He had no idea what Lucy would look like when she was old, especially not as old as the Crone seemed to be. He wanted to believe he would know his friend, his dearest friend, anywhere and anywhen but…

'Lucy, is it you?' he asked.

The Crone grinned. 'If it were, I'd never tell you.'

'Why?'

'Because I live to drive you nuts,' replied the old woman.

It was all the confirmation that Hobo needed.

In a blinding flash of light, Lucy and the shadow creature were once more aboard the creature's ship.

Lucy patted herself down. As best she could tell,

all of her was here.

The creature staggered left and right, unable to recompose itself.

'You fall apart in this world,' said Lucy. 'You disintegrate. You're not... compatible.'

'We will... optimise,' said the creature. It sounded like it was gasping, despite being too flat to possibly have lungs, and Lucy realised that wherever the creature's voice came from, it couldn't have been from its physical body. Another part of the Interface perhaps?

'Why did you even come here?' asked Lucy, 'Like this? Why a ship? Why London?'

'For you,' said the creature. 'For Lucy Wilson.'

'It's Lethbridge-Stewart these days,' said Lucy defiantly.

The creature, slowly composing itself, grew larger so that it towered even more over Lucy than it had done before. Its long, sharp fingers dragged against the floor, leaving tiny ripples in their wake.

'You... will never optimise. We have tried; we have tried so many times.'

Sounds like me,' said Lucy. 'It actually says "Not a team player" on my official file.'

'And so we optimised,' said the creature. 'We learnt that the Lucy Wilson Lethbridge-Stewart must choose.'

'Choose?'

'You will choose to optimise.'

'No,' said Lucy flatly. 'No way.'

She hoped she was being convincing. When she had been young, she had been 'Lucy Lethbridge-Stewart' every chance she'd had. She'd hunted out the weird, the strange, the dangerous. She believed it was her destiny, her duty, her inheritance. It was a long time before she realised that the right word, the word that perfectly described being the next in line to the Lethbridge-Stewart name was 'curse'.

'You will choose,' replied the creature. 'And you will help us.'

'Still no,' said Lucy. 'Instead, let me tell you what is going to happen if…'

'An excellent suggestion,' said the creature. 'Let us see what may happen.'

The creature whipped a hand towards Lucy, sending a ripple through the air. Lucy tried to dodge, but felt the icy cold of the Interface slam into her back, carrying her into darkness.

Lucy opened her eyes, realising instantly that she was once more in the Interface. She watched as she, another she, and Hobo ran across a field, explosions erupting on either side of them. Hobo had a new insignia on his uniform, a new rank. Behind them, more soldiers, all with the same insignia. Ahead of them, shrouded in smoke, dark shapes. Alien shapes.

'Don't fire until you see—' shouted Hobo, his voice cut off by the roar of another explosion, an explosion that tossed his body up into the air.

As the other Lucy ran to the spot where Hobo's body landed, Lucy observed a crumpled and lifeless heap. She watched as the other Lucy ripped the rank and insignia from Hobo's uniform and slapped it magnetically onto her own.

'Like the man said,' shouted other Lucy. 'Don't fire until you can see the eye stalk.

Lucy and the soldiers ran forward into darkness, leaving Hobo behind on the battlefield, and all the world went black.

Lucy opened her eyes, realising instantly that she was once more in the Interface. She saw herself, and Hobo, strapped to metal tables in a small room, struggling against leather straps that held them down tight. Around them, insectoid creatures in white robes scuttled around on four legs, dragging rusty old machinery across the room.

'Don't give them anything, Hobo,' said Lucy through gritted teeth. 'No matter what they do to me. Nothing's more important than protecting the Intelligence now.'

One of the creatures startled itself as it started up one of the machines with a mechanical belch and a cloud of greasy black smoke. Lucy heard the unmistakable sound of a saw blade spinning at high speed.

'They keep their ideas,' clicked one of the insect-men, 'inside their skull bone.'

'I get,' said another, heaving the rusty, whirling saw up in its front legs. 'Human skull bones soft.'

Lucy closed her eyes and covered her ears as the room filled with the sounds of a saw cutting into bone, and the sounds of Hobo screaming. She knew, of course, that the other Lucy would have no choice but to watch.

Lucy opened her eyes, realising instantly that she was once more in the Interface. Surrounded by flames, she watched as she and Hobo helped a group of soldiers load children into the back of army transport.

'Are they close, ma'am?' asked one of the soldiers.

'Too close,' said other Lucy, snatching a glimpse into the distance through some field binoculars. 'Damned Yetis, they'll never stop.'

'We need a distraction,' said Hobo. 'I'll slow them down so you can get to safety, work out our next move.'

'Hobo, you can't...'

I have to,' said Hobo. 'It's my fault, Lucy. I set them free.'

'Hobo, no!'

'I have to!'

Lucy watched as two of the soldiers grabbed her and, under Hobo's orders, forced her into the transport. She watched herself fight, and kick, and scream, and she watched as the transport drove away. She watched Hobo pull a chocolate bar out of his army fatigues and calmly munch on it as the enemy advanced. She watched the world go black once more.

Lucy opened her eyes, realising instantly that she was once more in the Interface.

'Stop!' she said, closing her eyes tightly. 'Just stop.'

'Do you understand now?'

The voice of the creature, either in her head or in her ear, it didn't matter which.

'Yes,' she said quietly. 'I understand.'

Another ripple, the icy feel of the Interface on her skin again, and a gasping lungful of the stale air of the ship told Lucy she was back. She opened her eyes, gingerly at first, then with a sigh of relief as she saw she was back on the alien ship.

On all fours, she touched the floor with trembling hands to ensure that it was real.

'I hate you,' she rasped. 'You should know that.'

'We will optimise,' replied the creature.

'I'm going to call you Goldilocks,' she said. 'I give

all my enemies' nicknames.'

'From the human story,' replied the creature. 'I understand.'

'How long?' asked Lucy. 'How long did you have me in there? I remember… so much.'

'By your reckoning,' replied the creature. 'Nearly three hundred years. Your capacity for watching your friend die is… quite remarkable. Please understand, none of those lives were optimal, but we had to find a way to make you understand. We must optimise, there will be consequences.'

'Why do I remember it?' asked Lucy. 'Only one of those lives can be real, so why do I remember them all?'

'Because you are Lucy Wilson,' said the creature. 'Lucy Wilson will not optimise.'

'Lucy Wilson must choose,' said Lucy. 'Lucy Wilson will choose.'

'This is good,' said the creature. 'You will help us, Lucy Wilson. You will help this universe to optimise.'

'One condition,' said Lucy, standing up. 'Hobo Kostinen.'

'He will be optimised,' replied the creature.

'In my way. I get to pick the time and the place you take me out of his life. Forever.'

'This,' replied the creature. 'Is optimal.'

*

The Crone and Hobo stood outside the Punch and Judy show.

'So, you're telling me you know that... thing?' asked Hobo incredulously.

'In a manner of speaking,' replied the Crone. 'It was my boss.'

'What?' shouted Hobo. 'How?'

'I took some persuading,' said the Crone. 'About three hundred years worth, as it goes.'

'What?' said Hobo, waving his hands around in frustration. 'Nothing you're saying makes sense!'

'Well, that's because you're not getting the story in the right order,' explained the Crone. 'Let's start with old shady from earlier, okay? It comes from outside this universe, from the Great Void. It wants to change this universe to make it compatible with itself, so it can enter. So it can take over. That's what it does.'

'Like terraforming?' asked Hobo. 'But the entire universe? All of... space?'

'Not just space. Time too,' replied the Crone.

'Is that why your ring stops them? Did you figure it out? Is it a time machine?'

'No,' said the Crone, 'I'm still not sure what it is, not entirely. But you can't go jumping around in time without creating paradoxes, and it does seem to keep me safe from those... or at least it did.'

The Crone held up her hand, which was clearly

devoid of rings.

'What happened?'

'It disappeared,' replied the Crone. 'Maybe it finally ran out of juice.'

'You realise that you've pretty much admitted to being Lucy, don't you?' said Hobo with a grin. 'That was her ring.'

'What a pity your only piece of evidence has disappeared,' retorted the Crone. 'Anyway, the point is that time's not a linear thing, and there is no time in the void, so that's the thing the creature understands the least. It makes changes, all through time, but it doesn't see the consequences coming.'

'I know all space-time,' said Hobo. 'Space-time is curved, shaped by mass and energy and...'

The Crone held up a hand. 'Slow down, professor. Let's just stick to "things don't always have to happen in order", okay? That's the important bit. Most things can happen or might happen or maybe won't ever happen but some things, some things always have to happen, more or less.'

'I was happy when time was a curved in eleven dimensions,' grumbled Hobo. 'You know where you are with eleven dimensions. I mean, Bosonic theory says twenty-seven but—'

'Would you pay attention? There are things that have to happen, Hobo. Things that no matter what that creature does, always have to happen. That's what's stopping it from turning the universe into what it needs it to be.'

'So what is it doing here? What were you doing for them?'

'Well, eventually they figured out that there were people, special people, who could interact with those "fixed points". People who were always there, always part of the story. People who could change things… just a little.'

'People like us?' said Hobo. The Crone winced; the note of excitement in Hobo's voice was unmistakable.

'People like me,' she said kindly. 'People who are always there when there's trouble. People the universe seems to… need? Like? I don't know. People like Lucy Wilson, I know that much. People like the Lethbridge-Stewarts.'

Hobo looked dejected. 'But not people like Hobo Kostinen…'

'No, not people like Hobo Kostinen. I'm sorry.'

Hobo shrugged.

'It's not a bad thing, you know. Your life can be… anything you want. You're a teenager who flies spaceships and battles aliens…'

'And how could anything be better than that?'

The Crone didn't answer, but the misty faraway look in her eye let Hobo know that there was an answer to his question; it just wasn't an answer that she was ready to give. Hobo wasn't sure it was an answer that he wanted to hear either.

'So, you worked for them?' he asked. 'You helped them?'

'It's a long story,' said the Crone, 'and it doesn't all happen in order.'

'So just tell me what happens next?'

The Crone patted Hobo on the shoulder reassuringly and lifted up the flap at the back of the Punch and Judy box.

'Now I steal your spaceship and leave you stranded and confused on Ogmore beach.'

'What?'

The Crone, half in and half out of the box, looked back over her shoulder with a grin on her face.

'Don't worry. If the next part of the story goes to plan, you won't remember this ever happened.'

Lucy stepped out of the Interface, back into the shadow creature's ship.

'It is done?' asked the creature.

'It's done, Goldilocks,' said Lucy grimly. 'Ogmore will never be the same. Another step closer to turning my universe into your perfect porridge.'

A ripple ran through the ship, reconfiguring it once again. Lucy had grown used to them now and she ignored it, pulling her gloves out of her pocket and slipping them back on before clasping her hands behind her back in an 'at ease' pose.

The creature stalked over to her, limbs stretching and shrinking as it poked and prodded itself into this world through the icy invisible barrier of the Interface.

'Optimisation,' it hissed gleefully. 'I can feel it. We can all feel it.'

'As long as he is safe,' said Lucy. 'Just tell me what I have to do next.'

The Punch and Judy box unfolded itself in almost exactly the same place it had been just seconds before, in the vast atrium of the Boneyard. Mad Jackson did a double take, not sure if the thing had disappeared and reappeared or not.

The Crone stepped out of the back, stretched the kinks out of her old bones, and gave Mad Jackson a wave.

'What sort of day we having, Jackson?' she asked.

'Short,' grunted Jackson.

'Good,' replied the Crone. 'I hate waiting around.'

Looking up at the clock, the Crone watched as the giant hand moved steadily forward, approaching the inevitable tock.

'Did you know that I designed this place, Jackson?' said the Crone.

'Eh?'

'The perfect prison, tagged on to the last second of available time, where nothing ever changes.' The Crone looked up at the clock again. 'At least, let's hope so. Any second now…'

And then, there it was. The tock, inexorable and inevitable, the very last moment of all possible time.

The Crone opened her eyes, as she always did, lying on her bed as she always was at the start of the day. She turned over and smiled. There it was – her staff, whole and complete, along with her metal band halfway down the shaft.

She jumped from the bed quickly, grabbing the staff, and hobbled over to the small desk and snatched up the Rubik's cube. With a half muttered prayer, she twisted it hard. It opened up, the top layer of cubes coming away, revealing a secret compartment hidden inside. A secret compartment that held a ring. A small, silver ring. A small silver ring that couldn't possibly be there, but was there all the same. A small silver ring that had been waiting there for a very long time. A small silver ring that an old woman had given a shadow creature – that wasn't a shadow creature at all – in a gift shop in Ogmore a long, long time ago. The Crone slipped it onto her finger and smiled before bringing her staff down hard on the desk, snapping it in two and catching the metal band that fell off it in her free hand. The same ring, in the same place, twice over. She slipped it onto her other hand. She could already feel energy moving between them, each battling the other, each treating the other as an aberration… a paradox.

The Crone took a deep breath. 'Okay,' she said to herself. 'Here we go.'

She strode out in the atrium. Above her, the clock ran quickly down from the tick to the tock.

The rattling began almost immediately, the invisible spirits of the Boneyard rushing across the atrium. They could sense something was different, and difference was never allowed here.

'Wakey wakey!' bellowed the Crone. 'Look lively, you horrible lot!'

On either side of her, doors in the atrium wall opened, the inmates of the Boneyard pouring out. They were all heroes, but heroes is a strange word. It can mean a lot of different things.

'Is it time?' asked Mad Jackson.

The Crone grinned. 'Oh yes,' she said with relish. 'Time is exactly what it is.'

Tables and chairs leapt into the air as the rattling spirits grew closer.

'Come on!' shouted the Crone. 'Let me look you in the eyes!'

The rattling grew louder, shaking the atrium. Inmates continued to pour in, banging on doors and waking up their neighbours.

'Form the circle!' ordered the Crone.

'You heard the lady!' bellowed Mad Old Jackson, taking a step forward. He reached out his huge arms and joined hands with the inmates from the rooms either side of his. Others followed suit, forming a circle around the outside of the atrium, disappearing from sight where the place vanished over its own horizon.

And then it came. The thing the Crone had been waiting for, oh, so very long.

A ripple. A change. A tear in the air right in front of her as a rattling spirit rose and forced its way through in the Boneyard. A black, formless thing that stretched and extruded and pulled itself into a form approaching human. Eyes that were not there, a mouth that contorted itself into the shape of a smile without being a smile at all.

'Hello, Goldilocks,' said the Crone.

'Hello, Lucy Wilson,' said the shadow creature.

Its eyes swivelled side to side, looking suspiciously at the circle of people that had formed around it. Countless people, drawn from points all across time and space, all united in this place and in this moment.

'Why have you summoned us here?' asked the creature. 'This place is the least optimal place of all.'

'I know,' said Lucy innocently. 'I made it,

remember?'

'We remember.'

'Fixed points in time, people who couldn't be optimised, that was the problem, wasn't it? You couldn't find a way to work around them, to make the universe what you needed it to be with them scattered all through time and space.'

'Until you corralled them here,' said the creature. 'And now we are able to optimise.'

'Except... you won't,' said Lucy. 'You see, the thing with time is, things don't always have to happen in order. There's a reason that you're outside of this universe – have you ever wondered why it is?'

'We do not wonder. To wonder is not optimal.'

'Well, I do. I wonder a lot. I daydream. I had this friend, a long time ago, now he was a thinker. Thinker with a big "T" if you know what I mean. He used to talk about this stuff all the time. Cause and effect. Causality. Paradoxes. He loved talking about paradoxes.'

'Optimisation has—'

'Consequences, I know,' said Lucy. 'But this time, the consequences are for you. What you do, reaching into our universe and moving people around like chess pieces – it's not right. Nobody should have that kind of power, to decide which lives are right and which are wrong, which choices we should and shouldn't make, who to save and who to leave to die. You are the worst possible monster of all – the monster that thinks it's right. The monster that doesn't know it's a monster at all.'

'You helped us,' said the creature defiantly.

'No,' said Lucy. 'I tricked you. You never really got your heads around time, and that was the weakness that I needed. You remember the first time I used the Interface, when I pulled myself out of Hobo's life?'

'Of course. You became optimal.'

'Yeah…' said Lucy. 'Kinda didn't, actually. Might have even lied a little bit.'

'Impossible!' snapped the creature. 'We knew optimisation. Your opposition to us was no longer an obstacle.'

Lucy held up her hands. One ring on each hand, each glowing white. The creature recoiled with a hiss, its form unravelling wherever the light from the rings touched it.

'What you felt was this,' explained Lucy. 'Two rings, but both the same ring, each one trying to protect me from the other. A walking paradox. Just like you, I couldn't exist. And if I couldn't exist, I couldn't be a problem, could I? That's what you felt.'

The creature staggered backwards, hissing, its arms tapering to sharp points that it raised in front of itself defensively.

'You have betrayed us.'

Lucy carefully pulled off the rings, holding each between a thumb and forefinger.

'You came to my world. You took away my friend. You tortured me. Betrayal is the least I could have done in return.'

Slowly, Lucy began to bring the rings together. They glowed brighter as they moved closer. Above her, the great clock began to shudder. The arm stopped, between the tick and the tock, spasming back and forth.

'I told you that I'd build you a prison at the end of time and fill it with all people who were like me. I just didn't tell you who the prison was for. I didn't tell you it was for you.'

'We have been optimising your universe ready for arrival since the dawn of time. You will not keep us out.'

'I already did,' said Lucy. 'That's the biggest paradox of all. I'm the one who casts you out. I'm the one you search for. I'm the one you think is going to help you, and I'm the one who casts you out again.'

Lucy took a step forward, then another, forcing the creature back.

'Look around,' she said, 'There's a reason I made this place a circle.'

The creature, its eyes narrowed to vicious slits, its mouth cracking into row after row of needle sharp teeth, let out an otherworldly howl. It was a sound of rage, and of anguish. It was a sound of infinite loneliness, unbearable jealousy, and endless hunger. It was the sound of the Great Void.

'You are the void. The void is you. I cast you out now, at the end, and at the very beginning of time.'

The creature lunged forward, its scissor fingers lancing towards Lucy's face.

Lucy brought the rings together. Two rings, overlapping, merging into each other to form a Moebius loop. The hand of the great clock leapt forward.

Tock.

Blinding light filled the Boneyard, a light so pure and so white that there was not a single shadow anywhere to be seen.

The Crone sat with Major Lucy Lethbridge-Stewart, sipping tea in an Ogmore tea room that hadn't been redecorated since some time in the early 1970s. As fixed points in time went, it was a definite candidate.

The Major checked her watch.

'She's late,' she grumbled.

'Of course she's late,' replied the Crone. 'So were you. So was I. It's a good sign. It means things are already going to plan.'

'What if she doesn't come?'

'She comes,' said the Crone, dunking a biscuit in

her tea. 'I remember, from when I was you. And from when I was her. So I know you, remember.'

The Major rolled her eyes. 'Good to know I end my life an insufferable smart-ass.'

'If you keep moaning, I'll tell you the exact time and date you lose your sense of humour.'

'Probably right around the time you told me I'm about to spend the rest of my life kidnapping people across the universe for evil creatures from another reality after being psychologically tortured for nearly three centuries.'

'Touché.'

The little bell above the tea room door rang before the major and the Crone could continue their conversation. Lucy Wilson walked in.

'I cannot remember being that young,' whispered the Crone.

'I can,' said the major. 'It was awful. I'd rather fight an entire battalion of Quarks single handed than go back to school.'

'You'll get your chance,' muttered the Crone, a crafty look in her eye.

The girl sat down opposite them, still in her school uniform. She pulled her hair loose and let it fall down around her face. Clearly, she didn't want to be seen.

'Tea, dear?' asked the Crone.

'I don't like tea,' replied Lucy.

'You will,' replied the major and the Crone.

'Mum's always telling me to have a word with myself,' grumbled Lucy. 'If she could see me now… Okay, future weird versions of me, what's up?'

And that was how it began, over tea and biscuits in a little tea shop that time might just have forgotten, in a little town on the edge of the sea. A plan that would take until the end of time, and back to the beginning again, to complete. A plan that needed three people who were all the same person, two rings, and a lot of luck.

A plan that would save everyone, everything, everywhere, and everywhen in the universe and that, if it worked, only a few people anywhere would ever know even a part of. Only one person, who was currently three people, would know the whole story, and even then not until the very end of her very long life.

The Major was the first to leave. She had a great many things to do and in some ways her road was the longest of all. The Crone's work was done and all Lucy had to do was wait, and to disappear when the time was right.

A fake disappearance, hidden amongst the time-meddlings of the Major and the shadow creature – the trigger for Hobo to reach out beyond the Earth for the most unlikely of help, and to journey even further in search of his lost friend. A friend who would come to Ogmore and face a monster that was herself, and pass a ring through space and time to create a paradox that was the final building block in a paradox so vast that none of this would ever happen at all.

'And you're sure I can't tell him?' young Lucy asked the Crone.

'Absolutely,' she replied. 'Hobo can't ever know. It's too much risk. If the plan fails....'

'But, what about those things... those things you said the creatures showed you. Do you think those really happen to him? Even one of them? I can't live with that.'

The Crone finished her tea with a loud slurp and stood up.

'I have to go,' she said. 'I have to persuade an insane alien to loan a schoolboy his magic time travelling box when he calls.'

She shuffled awkwardly around the table, leant down and whispered something in Lucy's ear.

Lucy smiled.

'I'll have to remember to tell myself that, right?' she asked.

'I don't know,' said the Crone. 'I didn't do it last time.'

And with that, she left, leaving Lucy with just the right number of unanswered questions.

Available from Candy Jar Books

Lost in Christmas by Michael Sloan

When the Karoller family visit Macy's on Christmas Eve, they are magically transported from the real world onto a series of Christmas cards.

As they jump from one card to another, they find themselves in Victorian England, meeting Elvis Presley, running away from dinosaurs, and making friends with a very clever smowman.

But how will they get home? In Lost in Christmas, the Karoller family learn life lessons about love, trust, family, and the spirit of Christmas.

Written by Michael Sloan (the man who created the TV series and Hollywood blockbuster *The Equalizer* featuring Denzel Washington). Other credits include: *Battlestar Galactica, Kung Fu: The Legend Continues, The Six Million Dollar Man, Alfred Hitchcock Presents, The Hardy Boys & Nancy Drew Mysteries* and *Columbo*.

Also available from Candy Jar Books

The Phoenix and the Carpet by E. Nesbit

The Phoenix and the Carpet is the sequel to E. Nesbit's beloved *Five Children and It*, and the second book in the Psammead trilogy.

When Cyril, Anthea, Robert, Jane and Lamb find a mysterious egg, the adventure of a lifetime begins.

With the help of their magical new friend, the Phoenix, the five siblings travel to exotic lands and befriend royalty, rescue treasures and meet one hundred and ninety-nine cats!

This heart-warming children's classic (featuring brand new illustrations by *Beano* artist Steve Beckett) is sure to delight readers young and old. Contains a foreword by Gary Russell, who played Cyril in the 1976 BBC TV serial.

Also available from Candy Jar Books

The Lucy Wilson Mysteries: Avatars of the Intelligence by Sue Hampton

Lucy Wilson doesn't want to move from London to sleepy South Wales. But when she arrives at her new seaside home, it doesn't appear to be as boring as she expected.

Ogmore-by-Sea seems to be under the control of a mysterious and powerful force. But why is Lucy its target? And why, when students at her new school start to disappear, does no one seem to care?

With the help of her new friend Hobo, Lucy Wilson must assume the mantle of her grandfather, the legendary Brigadier Lethbridge-Stewart, and defeat an invisible enemy before it's too late.

Also available from Candy Jar Books

The Lucy Wilson Mysteries: Curse of the Mirror Clowns by Chris Lynch

The circus is coming to town – and it may never leave.

Lucy Wilson is just about getting used to life in Ogmore-by-Sea. School, homework, friends, and the occasional alien... It's not easy being the new girl in town but, with the help of her steadfast companion Hobo, she's making it work.

But when a mysterious circus opens for one night only, the town suddenly finds itself overrun with invisible clowns and the gang are faced with their biggest mystery yet – the disappearance of Lucy Wilson herself.

Thankfully, they've got help – a mysterious stranger from another world with a special box that moves in time and space.

The Lucy Wilson Mysteries: The Midnight People by John Peel

Monknash was once home to a band of smugglers, but it is now dull and boring. Except to Greg Morton, who's absolutely terrified something unimaginable has happened to everyone in the village. He telephones his friend, Hobo, to ask for help.

When Hobo and Lucy arrive, they discover that something odd is definitely going on – but what? People seem joyless and dull, showing no emotions at all. Even Greg, who now insists that he was joking, seems very different.

Why are people walking toward the cliffs at the stroke of midnight? Who is the lady in the wheelchair? What are the villagers trying to protect in the caves? And why can't the local policeman see anything strange?

Can Lucy and Hobo take on an entire village by themselves?

The Lucy Wilson Mysteries: The Bandril Invasion by Wink Taylor

Billy Bandril is the TV sensation sweeping the nation! The hilarious antics of this anarchic puppet have kids and their parents waiting all week for another episode of mayhem.

Fresh from her latest adventure, Lucy Wilson could use some time relaxing in front of the box. But Hobo isn't too sure... There's something sinister about Billy and his influence over the viewing public.

When Lucy finds herself live on air with Billy, it's up to Hobo to interrupt the broadcast, before the curtains close... forever.

Will's War by Cherry Cobb

Will is an ordinary boy who likes to build Lego models and play with his dog, Rollo. But after a stupid row with his mum, he ends up at his grandad's house, where he discovers an old air raid shelter.

Will steps inside to investigate, but when he comes out he is not in his grandad's garden, but in Second World War London.

How will he get back?

The Norris Girls by Nigel Hinton

Dad is away in a dangerous place, but life must go on for the Norris girls.

Beth dreams of being in the school musical, especially when super cool Josh gets the lead part.

Georgy trains every day, trying to win a place in the Inter-Counties Athletics Championships but first she has to beat her arch-rival, Layla.

And Katie wants an animal to look after – a dog or a cat or a rabbit would do, but if she could choose one thing in the whole world it would be a pony.
Filled with tears and laughter, heartache and longing, this is Little Women for the twenty-first century.